# THE HUNGRY GODS OF CHICHEN ITZA

The chamber where Patricia lay captive must be near. Tarzan crept stealthily toward it—then was suddenly entangled in the meshes of a net dropped over him; a dozen warriors fell upon him and entangled him so that he was helpless.

With a priest blowing long blasts on a trumpet and awakening the city, he was carried down a long flight of steps. Now, focal point of a gaudy, barbaric night procession, he was led through the forest to the foot of a mountain, up which they zig-zagged until reaching the summit—the rim of the crater of an extinct volcano.

It was almost dawn as the procession wound its way down the crater and stopped at the edge of a yawning hole in its center.

Priests intoned a chant to the accompaniment of flutes, drums and trumpets; and, just as the sun rose, the net was cut away and Tarzan was hurled into the abyss.

COMPLETE AND UNABRIDGED!

# TARZAN
## and the
## Castaways

Edgar Rice Burroughs

BALLANTINE BOOKS • NEW YORK

ISBN 0-345-25964-5

This edition published by arrangement with
Edgar Rice Burroughs, Inc.

Manufactured in the United States of America

First U. S. Printing: July 1965
Fourth U. S. Printing: September 1977

First Canadian Printing: September 1965

Cover illustration by Boris Vallejo

# TABLE OF CONTENTS

# BIBLIOGRAPHIC NOTE

This book might be called *Last Adventures of Tarzan*. It is, perhaps, the last Tarzan book that will ever be published consisting of complete tales of the Ape Man written entirely by Edgar Rice Burroughs.

In 1963, thirteen years after ERB's death, Canaveral Press started issuing "new" Burroughs books, comprised of unpublished manuscripts and of magazine stories which had never appeared in book form. The first such volume was *Savage Pellucidar*, the seventh and final book in Burroughs' inner world series. Others that have followed (and are still in print) are *Tales of Three Planets*, *Tarzan and the Madman*, and *John Carter of Mars*.

The novel *Tarzan and the Castaways* is Edgar Rice Burroughs' original version of a story serialized in *Argosy* magazine in 1941 as *The Quest of Tarzan*. In addition to changing the name of the story, *Argosy's* editor also revised the text somewhat. The Canaveral edition uses the author's own manuscript as its source.

*Tarzan and the Champion* and *Tarzan and the Jungle Murders*, the shorter tales included in this volume, appeared originally in *Blue Book* and *Thrilling Adventures* magazines, both in 1940.

These three stories are the final adventures of Tarzan to appear in book form. There are no more complete Tarzan tales, but there remain in the hands of the author's family a fragmentary Tarzan manuscript left unfinished by Edgar Rice Burroughs. It is almost 25,000 words in length, or over half the length of an average novel. This fragment may someday be completed by a member of the Burroughs family, or by some other successor named by them.

If this should ever come about, *Tarzan and the Castaways* might better be called *Next-to-last Adventures of Tarzan*.

RICHARD A. LUPOFF
*Editor-in-Chief, Canaveral Press*
New York City,
November, 1964

# TARZAN
# AND
# THE CASTAWAYS

*

*

*

*

*

*

IT IS SOMETIMES DIFFICULT to know just where to begin a story. I recall an acquaintance of mine who, in telling of an accident wherein a neighbor had fallen down the cellar stairs and broken her leg, would recount all the marriages and deaths in the family for a generation or two back before getting to the point of the story.

In the present instance, I might go back to Ah Cuitok Tutul Xiu, the Mayan, who founded Uxmal in Yucatan in 1004 A.D.; and from him on to Chab Xib Chac, the Red Man, who destroyed Mayapan in 1451 and murdered the entire Cocom family of tyrants; but I shall not. I shall simply mention that Chac Tutul Xiu, a descendant of Ah Cuitok Tutul Xiu, motivated by that strange migratory urge of the Maya and by the advice of the Ah Kin Mai, or chief priest, left Uxmal with many of his followers, nobles, warriors, women, and slaves, and went to the coast where he constructed several large double dugout canoes and embarked therein upon the broad Pacific, never again to be heard of in his homeland.

That was in 1452 or 1453. From there I might make a broad calendric jump of some four hundred eighty-five or six years to modern times and to the island of Uxmal in the South Pacific, where Cit Coh Xiu is king; but I shall not do that either, since it would be anticipating my story.

Instead, I take you to the deck of the Saigon, a battered old tramp steamer awaiting at Mombasa to load wild animals for shipment to the United States. From below and from cages on deck come the plaints and threats of captured beasts; the deep-throated rumblings of lions, the trumpeting of elephants, the obscene "laugh" of hyenas, the chattering of monkeys.

At the rail two men are deep in argument: "But I tell you, Abdullah," one was saying, "we are practically ready to sail; the last consignment should be here within the week, and every day my expenses are mounting. It might take you a month to bring him in; you might not get him at all."

"I cannot fail, Sahib Krause," replied Abdullah Abu Néjm; "he has received an injury; that I know from Ndalo, in whose country he now is; and so he may be taken easily. Think of it, Sahib! A real wildman, raised by apes from infancy, the play fellow of elephants, the killer of lions. Wellah? he would be worth more than all your shipload of wild beasts in the land of the Nasara; he would make you a rich man, Sahib Krause."

"As I understand it, the fellow speaks English as well as the damned British themselves; I have heard of him for years. How long do you suppose I could exhibit in a cage in the United States a white man who can speak English? Abdullah, you are always saying that we Nasara are mad; I think it is you who are mad."

"You do not understand," replied the Arab. "This injury which he has suffered had deprived him of speech and the knowledge of speech; in that respect, he would be as your other beasts. They cannot complain, so that anyone can understand them; neither could he."

"Aphasia," muttered Krause.

"What did you say, Sahib?"

"That is the name of the affliction which has resulted in your man's loss of speech," explained Krause; "It is caused by a brain lesion. It puts a different aspect on the matter; the thing might be done—and very profitably; but yet—" He hesitated.

10

"You do not like the English, Sahib?" inquired Abdullah.

"I do not," snapped Krause. "Why do you ask?"

"This man is an Englishman," replied the Arab in his oiliest tones.

"What would you want for bringing him in?"

"The expenses of my safari, which would be very little, and the price of one lion."

"You do not ask much for so great a catch," commented Krause; "why is that? I expected you to rob me—as usual."

The Arab's eyes narrowed, and his sinister face seemed a mask of hate. "He is my enemy," he said.

"How long will it take?"

"Less than a month," replied Abdullah.

"I shall wait thirty days," said Krause; "then I shall sail, whether you are back or not."

\* \* \*

"I am bored," said the girl. "Mombasa! I hate it."

"You are always complaining," growled Krause; "I don't know why the devil I brought you along; anyway, we sail in three days, whether that Arab dog is back or not; then I suppose you'll find something else to grouse about."

"It must be a very valuable specimen Abdullah is bringing you," said the girl.

"It is."

"What is it, Fritz—a pink elephant or a crimson lion?"

"It is a wild man, but keep it to yourself—the English pigs would never let me take him aboard, if they knew."

"A wild man! One of those whose heads come up to a little point on top, like a cone? He should have a little tuft of hair right on the tip top of the cone, and his nose should spread all across his face, and he shouldn't have any chin. Is he like that, Fritz?"

"I have never seen him, but I suppose he is just like that—that has been orthodox ever since Barnum's What-is-it."

"Look, Fritz! Here comes Abdullah now."

The swart Arab came over the side and approached them; his face betokened nothing of either the success or failure of his mission.

11

"Marhaba!" Krause greeted him. "Ey khabar?"

"The best of tidings, Sahib," replied Abdullah. "I have him, just outside of town, in a wooden cage covered with matting, so that none may see what is within; but billah! what a time we had in capturing him! We took him in a net, but he killed three of Ndalo's warriors before they could tie his hands behind him. He is strong as el-fil. We have had to keep his hands tied ever since we got him: he would have torn that wooden cage to pieces in an instant, had we not."

"I have an iron cage that he cannot tear to pieces," said Krause.

"I would not be too sure of that," cautioned the Arab. "If your cage could not withstand the strength of el-fil, you had still better keep his hands tied."

"My cage would not hold an elephant," said Krause, "but if it could, it would be strong enough."

"I would still keep his hands tied," persisted Abdullah.

"Has he spoken?" asked Krause.

"No; not a word—he just sits and looks. There is neither hate nor fear in his eyes—he reminds me of el adrea; I am always expecting to hear him roar. We have to feed him by hand, and when he eats his meat, he growls like el adrea."

"Wonderful!" exclaimed Krause. "He will be a sensation. I can just see those fool Americans begging to pay good money to see him. Now listen—I shall clear this afternoon and stand up the coast, returning after dark. Load the cage on a dhow below the town and stand straight out until you pick up my signal—I'll blink my running light three times in rapid succession at intervals; then you show a light. Do you understand?"

"It is already done," said Abdullah Abu Néjm.

*　　*　　*

The wind had risen and a sea was running when Abdullah picked up the Saigon's signal. Maneuvering the dhow into position along the lee side of the steamer was finally accomplished. Tackle was lowered and made fast to the cage containing the wild man. Abdullah was guiding the cage as it was hoisted from the dhow, when suddenly the Saigon

12

rolled over away from the smaller craft; the cage was jerked suddenly upward; and Abdullah, fearing that he would be hurled into the sea, clung to it. The cage crashed against the side of the steamer; the men above continued to hoist; then the Saigon rolled back and crashed down upon the dhow, swamping it.

All of the crew of the dhow were lost, and Abdullah was aboard the steamer bound for America. He filled the air with "billahs!" and "Wullah-bullahs!" and called upon Allah to preserve him.

"You're damn lucky to be alive," Krause told him. "You'll make a lot of money in America. I'll exhibit you, too, as the shiek who captured the wild man; they'll pay plenty to see a real shiek straight from the desert. I'll buy a camel for you, and you can ride through the streets with a banner advertising the show."

"I, Abdullah Abu Néjm, exhibited like a wild beast!" screamed the Arab. "Never!"

Krause shrugged. "Have it your own way," he said; "but don't forget, you got to eat, and you won't find many free date trees in America. I'll feed you until we get there, but after that you're on your own."

"Dog of a Nasrany!" muttered the Arab.

## II

The following morning was fair, with a brisk wind, as the Saigon steamed northeastward across the Indian Ocean. The animals on deck were quiet. A wooden cage, entirely covered with matting, was lashed down amidships. No sound came from it, either.

Janette Laon followed Krause on deck; her black hair was blowing in the wind, which pressed her light dress against her, revealing a figure of exceptional allure. Wilhelm Schmidt, the 2nd mate of the Saigon, leaning with his back against the rail, watched her through half-closed eyes.

"Now may I see your wild man, Fritz?" asked the girl.

"I hope he's still alive," said the man; "he must have got an awful beating when we hauled him aboard last night."

"Haven't you tried to find out?" she demanded.

"Couldn't have done anything for him, anyway," replied Krause. "From what Abdullah told me, he'd be a mean customer to handle. Come on; we'll have a look at him. Hey, you!" he called to a Lascar sailor; "take the matting off that cage."

As they watched the man at work, Schmidt came over and joined them. "What you got in there, Mr. Krause?" he asked.

"A wild man; ever see one?"

"I saw a Frenchie once, whose wife had run off with the chauffeur," said Schmidt; "he sure was a wild man."

The sailor had removed the lashings, and now he dragged away the matting. Inside the cage, a giant figure squatted on his haunches, appraising them with level gaze.

"Why, he's a white man!" exclaimed the girl.

"So he is," said Krause.

"You goin' to keep a man penned up in a cage like a beast?" asked Schmidt.

"He's only white on the outside," said Krause—"he's an Englishman."

Schmidt spat into the cage. The girl stamped her foot angrily. "Don't ever do that again," she said.

"What's he to you?" demanded Krause. "Didn't you hear me say he's nothing but a dirty English pig."

"He's a human being and a white man," replied the girl.

"He's a dummy," retorted Krause; "can't speak a word nor understand one. It's an honor for him to be spit on by a German."

"Nevertheless, don't let Schmidt do it again."

The ship's bell sounded, and Schmidt went to relieve the 1st mate on the bridge.

"He's the pig," said the girl, looking after Schmidt.

The two stood looking at the wild man as Hans de Groote came down from the bridge and joined them. The Dutchman was a goodlooking young fellow in his early twenties; he had been signed on as 1st mate at Batavia on the trip out, after his predecessor had mysteriously "fallen overboard." Schmidt, who thought that he should have had the assignment, hated him and made no effort to conceal the fact. That there was bad blood between them was nothing to cause comment aboard the Saigon, for bad blood was the rule rather than the exception.

Larsen, the captain, who was now confined to his cabin with a bad attack of fever, was not on speaking terms with Krause, who had chartered the ship; while the crew, made up principally of Lascars and Chinese, were always on the verge of knifing one another. On the whole, the captive beasts were the most admirable creatures aboard.

De Groote stood looking at the man in the cage for several seconds before he spoke. His reaction was almost identical with that of the girl and Schmidt. "He's a white man!" he exclaimed. "You're certainly not going to keep him in a cage like a wild beast!"

"That's exactly what I'm going to do," snapped Krause, "and it's none of your damned business, nor any one else's"; and he shot a scowling glance at the girl.

"He's your wild man," said de Groote, "but at least free his hands; it's unnecessary cruelty to keep him tied up like that."

"I'm going to free his hands," said Krause, grudgingly, "as

15

soon as I can get an iron cage up from below; it would be too much of a job feeding him this way."

"He's had nothing to eat or drink since yesterday," said the girl. "I don't care what he is, Fritz; I wouldn't treat a dog the way you're treating this poor man."

"Neither would I," retorted Krause.

"He is less than a dog," said a voice behind them. It was the voice of Abdullah Abu Néjm. He came close to the cage and spat on the man within, and the girl slapped Abdullah Abu Néjm across the face with all her strength. The Arab's hand flew to his dagger, but de Groote stepped between the two and seized the man's wrist.

"You shouldn't have done that, Janette," said Krause.

The girl's eyes were flashing fire, and the blood had left her face. "I'll not stand by and see him insult that man," she said; "and that goes for the rest of you, too"; and she looked straight into Krause's eyes.

"And I'll back her up," said de Groote. "Maybe it's none of my business if you keep him in a cage, but I'll make it some of my business if you don't treat him decently. Have you ordered the iron cage up yet?"

"I'll treat him as I please," said Krause; "and what are you going to do about it?"

"I'll beat hell out of you," replied de Groote, "and then turn you in to the authorities at the first port of call."

"Here comes the iron cage now," said Janette. "Get him into it and take those cords off his wrists."

Krause was frightened at de Groote's threat to notify the authorities; that made him squirm. "Oh, come," he said in mollifying tones, "I'm going to treat him all right. I got a lot of money tied up in him and I expect to make a lot out of him; I'd be a fool not to treat him well."

"See that you do," said de Groote.

A big iron cage was swung up from below and placed close to the wooden cage, the two doors close together. Krause drew a revolver; then both doors were raised. The man in the wooden cage did not move.

"Get in there, you dumb idiot!" yelled Krause, pointing the revolver at the man. He did not even look at Krause.

"Get a capstan bar, one of you men," directed Krause, "and poke him from behind."

"Wait," said the girl; "let me try." She walked to the opposite side of the iron cage and beckoned to the captive. He just looked at her. "Come here a minute," she said to de Groote; "let me take your knife; now place your wrists together, as though they were bound; yes, that's it." She took the knife and pretended to sever imaginary cords about de Groote's wrists; then she beckoned again to the man in the wooden cage. He arose, but still stooped, as he could not stand erect in the small wooden cage, and walked into the larger cage.

The girl was standing close to the bars, the knife in her hand; a sailor dropped the door of the iron cage; the captive approached the girl and, turning his back toward her, pressed his wrists against the bars.

"You said he was stupid," Janette said to Krause; "he's not stupid; I could tell that by just looking at him." She cut the bonds from his wrists, which were discolored and swollen. The man turned and looked at her. He said nothing, but his eyes seemed to thank her.

De Groote was standing beside Janette. "He's a fine-looking specimen, isn't he?" he said.

"And handsome," said the girl. She turned to Krause. "Have some water and food brought," she directed.

"You going to be his nurse maid?" inquired Krause with a sneer.

"I'm going to see that he's treated decently," she replied. "What does he eat?"

"I don't know," replied Krause. "What *does* he eat, Abdullah?"

"The dog has not eaten for two days," replied the Arab; "so I guess he will eat almost anything. In the jungle he eats raw meat from his kills, like a beast."

"We'll try him on some," said Krause; "it will be a good way of getting rid of any of the animals that die." He sent a sailor to the galley for meat and water.

The man in the iron cage looked long at Abdullah Abu Néjm; so long that the Arab spat on the deck and turned away.

17

"I wouldn't want to be in your shoes if he ever got out of that cage," said Krause,

"You should not have freed his hands," said Abdullah; "he is more dangerous than the lion."

When the sailor returned with the meat and water, Janette took them from him and passed them in to the wild man. He took a small swallow of water; then he went into a far corner of his cage, squatted on his haunches, and tore at the meat with his strong, white teeth; and as he ate, he growled.

The girl shuddered, and the men moved about uneasily. "El adrea of the broad head eats thus," said Abdullah.

"He sounds like a lion," said Krause. "By what name do the natives know him, Abdullah?"

"He is called Tarzan of the Apes," replied the Arab.

# III

The Saigon crossed the Indian Ocean to Sumatra, where Krause took on two elephants, a rhinoceros, three orangutans, two tigers, a panther, and a tapir. Fearing that de Groote would make good his threat to report the human captive to the authorities at Batavia, Krause did not put in there as he had intended; but continued on to Singapore for monkeys, another tiger, and several boa constrictors; then the Saigon steamed across the South China Sea toward Manila, its last port of call on the long drag to the Panama Canal.

Krause was delighted; so far all his plans had worked out splendidly; and if he got his cargo to New York, he stood to clean up an excellent profit. Perhaps he would not have been so delighted had he known of all that went on aboard the Saigon. Larsen was still confined to his cabin, and while de Groote was a good officer, he was young, and new aboard the ship. Like Krause, he did not know all that was talked of in the forecastle and on deck at night when it was Schmidt's watch. At such times, the 2nd mate spoke long and earnestly with Jabu Singh, the Lascar; and he spoke in whispers. Afterward, Jabu Singh spoke long and earnestly with the other Lascars in the forecastle.

"But the wild beasts?" asked Chand of his fellow Lascar, Jabu Singh; "what of them?"

"Schmidt says we throw them overboard along with de Groote, Krause, and the others."

"They are worth much money," objected Chand; "we should keep them and sell them."

"We should be caught and hanged," said another Lascar.

"No," Jabu Singh contradicted. "While we were in Singapore, Schmidt learned that Germany and England have gone to war. This is an English ship; Schmidt says that a German has a right to capture it. He says we would get prize money; but he thinks the animals would be valueless, and they are a nuisance."

19

"I know a man on the island of Illili who would buy them," said Chand. "We will not let Schmidt throw them overboard."

The men spoke in their native dialect, confident that the Chinese sailors would not understand them; but in that they were wrong; Lum Kip had once sailed the China Sea aboard a felucca that had been captained and manned by Lascars, and he had learned their language. He had also learned to hate Lascars, as he had been treated very badly aboard the felucca and had been given no share of the spoils of their nefarious operations. But Lum Kip's face gave no indication that he understood what he overheard; it wore its usual expression of profound detachment, as he puffed on his long pipe with its little brass bowl.

The man in the large iron cage on deck often paced back and forth for hours at a time. Often he leaped and seized the bars at the top of the cage and swung to and fro from one end of the cage to the other, hand over hand. When anyone approached his cage, he would stop; for he was not doing these things for his amusement, nor for the amusement of others, but to keep his magnificent physique from deteriorating during his confinement.

Janette Laon came often to his cage; she saw that he was fed regularly and that he always had water; and she tried to teach him her native language, French; but in this she made no headway. Tarzan knew what was the matter with him; and while he could neither speak nor understand speech, his thoughts were as coherent and intelligent as ever. He wondered if he would ever recover; but he was not greatly troubled because he could not converse with human beings; the thing that annoyed him most was that he could no longer communicate with manu, the monkey, or the mangani, the great apes, with which he classed the orang-utans that were aboard and confined in cages near his. Seeing the cargo that the Saigon carried, he knew the life that lay in store for him; but he also knew that sooner or later he would escape. He thought of that most often when he saw Abdullah Abu Néjm on deck.

He had tested the bars of his cage at night when nobody was near; and he was confident that he could spread them sufficiently to allow his body to pass between them; but he guessed that were he to do so, while at sea, he would only be shot down; for he knew that they feared him. With the patience of a wild beast he bided his time.

When Abdullah Abu Néjm or Schmidt were on deck, his eyes followed them; for these two had spat at him. Abdullah Abu Néjm had reason to hate him, for Tarzan had ended his lucrative career as a slave trader and ivory poacher; but the 2nd mate had been motivated only by the natural reactions of a bully and a coward who discovers one whom he considers his racial enemy powerless to retaliate.

Abdullah Abu Néjm, hating Krause and the girl and ignored by de Groote, consorted much with Schmidt, until the two men, finding much in common, became boon companions. Abdullah, glad of any opportunity to wreak vengeance on Krause, willingly agreed to aid Schmidt in the venture the 2nd mate was planning.

"The Lascars are with me to a man," Schmidt told Abdullah, "but we haven't approached the chinks; there's bad blood between them and the Lascars on this ship, and Jabu Singh says his men won't play if the chinks are to be in on it and get a cut."

"There are not many," said Abdullah, "If they make trouble, they, too, can go overboard."

"The trouble is, we need 'em to man the ship," explained Schmidt; "and about throwing 'em overboard; I've changed my mind; there ain't anybody going overboard. They're all going to be prisoners of war; then, if anything goes wrong, there's no murder charge against us."

"You can run the ship without Larsen and de Groote?" asked the Arab.

"Sure I can," replied Schmidt. "I've got Oubanovitch on my side. Being a Red Russian, he hates Krause; he hates everybody who has a pfennig more than he. I'm making him 1st mate, but he'll have to keep on running the engine room too. Jabu Singh will be 2nd mate. Oh, I've got everything worked out."

"And you are to be captain?" inquired the Arab.

"Certainly."

"And what am I to be?"

"You? Oh, hell, you can be admiral."

That afternoon Lum Kip approached de Groote. "Maybe-so you make dead tonight," said Lum Kip in a low whisper.

"What you driving at, Lum?" demanded de Groote.

"You savvy Schmidt?"

"Of course; what about him?"

"Tonight he takee ship; Lascars, they takee ship; 'banovitchee, he takee ship; man in long, white dless, he takee ship. They killee Larsen; killee you; killee Klause; killee evlybody. Chinee boy no takee ship; no killee. You savvy?"

"You having a pipe dream, Lum?" demanded de Groote.

"No pipe dleam: you waitee see."

"How about Chinee boys?" asked de Groote, who was now thoroughly worried.

"They no killee you."

"Will they fight Lascar boys?"

"You betee; you give 'em gun."

"No have gun," said de Groote; "tell 'em get capstan bars, belaying pins; knives. You savvy?"

"Me savvy."

"And when the trouble starts, you boys light into the Lascars."

"You betee."

"And thank you, Lum; I'll not forget this."

De Groote went at once to Larsen; but found him rolling on his bunk, delirious with fever; then he went to Krause's cabin, where he found Krause and Janette Laon and explained the situation to them.

"Do you believe the Chink?" asked Krause.

"There's no reason for him to have made up such a cock-and-bull story," replied de Groote; "yes, I believe him; he's one of the best hands on the ship—a quiet little fellow who always does his work and minds his own business."

"What had we better do?" asked Krause.

"I'll put Schmidt under arrest immediately," said de Groote.

The cabin door swung open; and Schmidt stood in the doorway, an automatic in his hand. "Like hell, you'll put me under arrest, you damned Dutchman," he said. "We saw that dirty little Chink talking to you, and we had a pretty good idea what he saying."

Half a dozen Lascars pressed behind Schmidt, outside the doorway. "Tie 'em up," he said to them.

The sailors brushed past Schmidt into the cabin; de Groote stepped in front of the girl. "Keep your dirty hands off her," he said to the Lascars. One of them tried to push him aside and reach Janette, and de Groote knocked him down. Instantly there was a free-for-all; but only de Groote and Janette took part in it on their side; Krause cowered in a corner and submitted fearfully to having his hands tied behind his back. Janette picked up a pair of heavy binoculars and felled one of the Lascars while de Groote sent two more to the floor, but the odds were against them. When the fight was over, they were both trussed up and de Groote was unconscious from a blow on the head.

"This is mutiny, Schmidt," said Krause; "you'll hang for this if you don't let me go."

"This is not mutiny," replied Schmidt. "This is an English ship, and I'm taking it in the name of our Fuhrer."

"But I'm a German," Krause objected; "I chartered this ship—it is a German Ship."

"Oh, no," said Schmidt; "it is registered in England, and you sail it under English colors. If you're a German, then you're a traitor, and in Germany we know what to do with traitors."

# IV

Tarzan knew that something had happened aboard the ship, but he did not know what. He saw a Chinese sailor strung up by the thumbs and lashed. For two days he saw nothing of the girl or the young 1st mate, and now he was not fed regularly or kept supplied with water. He saw that the 2nd mate, who had spit on him, was in command of the ship; and so, while he did not know, he surmised what had happened. Abdullah Abu Néjm occasionally passed his cage, but without molesting him; and Tarzan knew why—the Arab was afraid of him, even though he were penned up in an iron cage. He would not always be in a cage: Tarzan knew this and Abdullah Abu Néjm feared it.

Now, Lascars swaggered about the ship and the Chinese did most of the work. These, Schmidt cuffed and kicked on the slightest provocation or on none at all. Tarzan had seen the man who had been strung up by his thumbs and lashed cut down after an hour and carried to the forecastle. The cruelty of the punishment disgusted him, but of course he did not know but that the man deserved it.

The 2nd mate never passed Tarzan's cage without stopping to curse him. The very sight of Tarzan seemed to throw him into a fit of uncontrollable rage, as did anything that stimulated his inferiority complex. Tarzan could not understand why the man hated him so; he did not know that Schmidt, being a psychopath, did not have to have a reason for anything that he did.

Once he came to the cage with a harpoon in his hands and jabbed it through the bars at the ape-man while Abdullah Abu Néjm looked on approvingly. Tarzan seized the haft and jerked the thing from Schmidt's hands as effortlessly as he might have taken it from a baby. Now that the wild man was armed, Schmidt no longer came close to the cage.

On the third day from that on which he had last seen the girl, Tarzan saw his wooden cage and a larger iron cage hoisted to the deck and lashed down near his; and a little later he saw the girl led on deck by a couple of Lascar sailors and put into the wooden cage; then de Groote and Krause were brought up and locked in the iron cage, and presently Schmidt came from the bridge and stopped in front of them.

"What is the meaning of this, Schmidt?" demanded de Groote.

"You complained about being locked up below, didn't you? You should thank me for having you brought on deck instead of finding fault. You'll get plenty of fresh air up here and a good tan; I want you all to look your best when I exhibit you with the other specimens of the lower orders in Berlin," and Schmidt laughed.

"If you want to amuse yourself by keeping Krause and me penned up here like wild beasts, go ahead; but you can't mean that you're going to keep Miss Laon here, a white woman exhibited before a lot of Lascar sailors." It had been with difficulty that de Groote had kept his anger and contempt from being reflected in his voice, but he had long since come to the conclusion that they were in the hands of a madman and that to antagonize him further would be but to add to the indignities he had already heaped upon them.

"If Miss Laon wishes to, she may share the captain's cabin with me," replied Schmidt; "I have had Larsen taken elsewhere."

"Miss Laon prefers the cage of a wild animal," said the girl.

Schmidt shrugged. "That is a good idea," he said; "I shall see about putting you into the cage of one of Herr Krause's lions, or perhaps you would prefer a tiger."

"Either one, to you," replied the girl.

"Or maybe into the cage with the wild man you have been so fond of," suggested Schmidt; "that might afford a spectacle all would enjoy. From what Abdullah tells me, the man is probably a cannibal. I shall not feed him after I put you in with him."

Schmidt was laughing to himself as he walked away.

"The man is absolutely crazy," said de Groote. "I have known right along that he was a little bit off, but I never suspected that he was an out-and-out madman."

"Do you suppose that he will do what he has threatened?" asked Janette.

Neither de Groote nor Krause replied, and their silence answered her questions and confirmed her own fears. It had been all right to feed the wild man and see that he had water, but she had always been ready to spring away from his cage if he attempted to seize her. She had really been very much afraid of him, but her natural kindness had prompted her to befriend him. Furthermore, she had known that it annoyed Krause, whom she secretly detested.

Stranded in Batavia, Janette had seized upon Krause's offer so that she might get away, anywhere; and the prospect of New York had also greatly intrigued her. She had heard much of the great American metropolis and fabulous stories of the ease with which a beautiful girl might acquire minks and sables and jewels there, and Janette Laon knew that she would be beautiful in any country.

Although neither de Groote nor Krause had answered Janette's question, it was soon answered. Schmidt returned with several sailors; he and two of the Lascars were armed with pistols, and the others carried prod poles such as were used in handling the wild animals.

The sailors unlashed Janette's cage and pushed it against that in which Tarzan was confined, the two doors in contact; then they raised both doors.

"Get in there with your wild man," ordered Schmidt.

"You can't do that, Schmidt," cried de Groote. "For God's sake man, don't do a thing like that!"

"Shut up!" snapped Schmidt. "Get in there wench! Poke her up with those prods, you!"

One of the Lascars prodded Janette, and Tarzan growled and started forward. Three pistols instantly covered him, and sharp pointed prods barred his way. The growl terrified the girl; but, realizing that they could force her into the cage, she suddenly walked in boldly, her chin up. The iron gate of the cage dropped behind her, the final seal upon her doom.

De Groote, Krause, Schmidt, and the Lascars awaited in breathless silence for the tragedy they anticipated with varying emotions: Schmidt pleasurably, the Lascars indifferently, Krause nervously, and de Groote with such emo-

26

tions as his phlegmatic Dutch psyche had never before experienced. Had he been a Frenchman or an Italian, he would probably have screamed and torn his hair; but, being a Dutchman, he held his emotions in leash within him.

Janette Laon stood just within the doorway of the cage, waiting; she looked at Tarzan and Tarzan looked at her. He knew that she was afraid, and he wished that he might speak to her and reassure her; then he did the only thing that he could; he smiled at her. It was the first time that she had seen him smile. She wanted to believe that it was a reassuring smile, a friendly smile; but she had been told such terrible stories of his ferocity that she was uncertain; it might be a smile of anticipation. To be on the safe side, she forced an answering smile.

Tarzan picked up the harpoon he had taken from Schmidt and crossed the cage toward her. "Shoot him, Schmidt!" shouted de Groote; "he is going to kill her."

"You think I am crazy?—to kill a valuable exhibit like that!" replied Schmidt. "Now we see some fun."

Tarzan handed the harpoon to the girl, and went back and sat down at the far end of the cage. The implication of the gesture was unmistakable. Janette felt her knees giving from beneath her; and sat down quickly, lest she fall. Sudden relief from terrific nervous strain often induces such a reaction. De Groote broke into a violent sweat.

Schmidt fairly jumped up and down in rage and disappointment. "Wild man!" he shrieked. "I thought you said that thing was a wild man, Abdullah. You are a cheat! You are a liar!"

"If you don't think he's a wild man, Nasrany," replied the Arab, "go yourself into his cage."

Tarzan sat with his eyes fixed on Schmidt. He had understood nothing that the man had said; but from his facial expressions, his gestures, his actions, and by all that had occurred, he had judged the man; another score was chalked up against Herr Schmidt; another nail had been driven into his coffin.

# V

The next morning the two captives in the big iron cage were very happy. Janette was happy because she found herself safe and unharmed after a night spent with a creature who ate his meat raw and growled while he ate, a wild man who had killed three African warriors with his bare hands before they could overpower him, and whom Abdullah accused of being a cannibal. She was so happy that she sang a snatch of a French song that had been popular when she left Paris. And Tarzan was happy because he understood the words; while he had slept his affliction had left him as suddenly as it had struck.

"Good morning, he said in French, the first human language he had ever learned, taught to him by the French lieutenant he had saved from death on a far gone day.

The girl looked at him in surprise. "I—good morning!" she stammered. "I—I—they told me you could not speak."

"I suffered an accident," he explained; "I am all right now."

"I am glad," she said; "I—" she hesitated.

"I know," interrupted Tarzan; "you were afraid of me. You need not be."

"They said terrible things about you; but you must have heard them."

"I not only could not speak," Tarzan explained, "but I could not understand. What did they say?"

"They said that you were very ferocious and that you—you—ate people."

Again one of Tarzan's rare smiles. "And so they put you in here hoping that I would eat you? Who did that?"

"Schmidt, the man who led the mutiny and took over the ship."

"The man who spit on me," said Tarzan, and the girl thought that she detected the shadow of a growl in his voice. Abdullah had been right; the man did remind one of a lion. But now she was not afraid.

"You disappointed Schmidt," she said. "He was furious when you handed me the harpoon and went to the other end of the cage and sat down. In no spoken language could one have assured him of my safety more definitely."

"Why does he hate you?"

"I don't know that he does hate me; he is a sadistic maniac. You must have seen what he did to poor Lum Kip and how he kicks and strikes others of the Chinese sailors."

"I wish you would tell me what has gone on aboard the ship that I have not been able to understand and just what they intend doing with me, if you know."

"Krause was taking you to America to exhibit as a wild man along with his other—I mean along with his wild animals."

Again Tarzan smiled. "Krause is the man in the cage with the 1st mate?"

"Yes."

"Now tell me about the mutiny and what you know of Schmidt's plans."

When she had finished, Tarzan had every principal in the drama of the Saigon definitely placed; and it seemed to him that only the girl, de Groote, and the Chinese sailors were worthy of any consideration—they and the caged beasts.

De Groote awoke, and the first thing that he did was to call to Janette from his cage. "You are all right?" he asked. "He didn't offer to harm you?"

"Not in any way," she assured him.

"I'm going to have a talk with Schmidt today and see if I can't persuade him to take you out of that cage. I think that if Krause and I agree never to prefer charges against him, if he lets you out, he may do it."

"This is the safest place on the ship for me; I don't want to get out as long as Schmidt is in control."

De Groote looked at her in astonishment. "But that fellow is half beast," he exclaimed. "He may not have harmed you yet; but you never can tell what he might do, especially if Schmidt starves him as he has threatened."

Janette laughed. "You'd better be careful what you say about him if you think he is such a ferocious wild man; he might get out of this cage some time."

"Oh, he can't understand me," said de Groote; "and he can't get out of the cage."

Krause had been awakened by the conversation, and now he came and stood beside de Groote. "I'll say he can't get out of that cage," he said, "and Schmidt will see that he never gets the chance; Schmidt knows what he would get, and you needn't worry about his understanding anything we say; he's as dumb as they make 'em."

Janette turned to look at Tarzan to note the effect of de Groote's and Krause's words, wondering if he would let them know that he did understand and was thoroughly enjoying the situation. To her surprise she saw that the man had lain down close to the bars and was apparently asleep; then she saw Schmidt approaching and curbed her desire to acquaint de Groote and Krause with the fact that their wild man could have understood everything they said, if he had heard them.

Schmidt came up to the cage. "So you are still alive," he said. "I hope you enjoyed your night with the monkey man. If you will teach him some tricks, I'll exhibit you as his trainer." He moved close to the cage and looked down at Tarzan. "Is he asleep, or did you have to kill him?"

Suddenly Tarzan's hand shot between the bars and seized one of Schmidt's ankles; then the ape man jerked the leg into the cage its full length, throwing Schmidt upon his back. Schmidt screamed, and Tarzan's other hand shot and plucked the man's pistol from its holster.

"Help!" screamed Schmidt. "Abdullah! Jabu Singh! Chand! Help!"

Tarzan twisted the leg until the man screamed again from pain. Abdullah, Jabu Singh, and Chand came running in answer to Schmidt's cries; but when they saw that the wild man was pointing a pistol in their direction, they stopped.

"Have food and water brought, or I'll twist your leg off," said Tarzan.

"The dog of an Engleys speaks!" muttered Abdullah. De Groote and Krause looked in amazement.

"If he speaks, he must have understood us," said Krause. "Maybe he has understood all along," Krause tried to recall what he might have said that some day he might regret, for

30

he knew that the man could not be kept in a cage forever—unless. But the fellow had a gun now; it would not be so easy to kill him. He would speak to Schmidt about it; it was as much to Schmidt's interests as his now to have the man put out of the way.

Schmidt was screaming for food and water. Suddenly de Groote cried, "Look out, man! Look out! Behind you!" But it was too late; a pistol spoke, and Tarzan collapsed upon the floor of the cage, Jabu Singh had crept up behind the cage, unnoticed until the thing had been done.

Schmidt scrambled out of the way, but Janette recovered the pistol; and, turning, shot Jabu Singh as he was about to fire another shot into the prostrate man. Her shot struck the Lascar in the right arm, causing him to drop his weapon; then, keeping him covered, the girl crossed the cage, reached through the bars, and retrieved Jabu Singh's pistol. Now, she crossed back to Tarzan, knelt above him, and placed her ear over his heart.

As Schmidt stood trembling and cursing in impotent fury, a ship was sighted from the bridge; and he limped away to have a look at it. The Saigon was running without colors, ready to assume any nationality that Schmidt might choose when an emergency arose.

The stranger proved to be an English yacht; so Schmidt ran up the English flag; then he radioed, asking if they had a doctor on board, as he had two men suffering from injuries, which was quite true; at least Jabu Singh was suffering, with vocal accompaniment; Tarzan still lay where he had fallen.

The yacht had a doctor aboard, and Schmidt said that he would send a boat for him. He, himself, went with the boat, which was filled with Lascars armed with whatever they could find, a weird assortment of pistols, rifles, boat hooks, knives, and animal prods, all well hidden from sight.

Coming alongside the yacht, they swarmed up the Jacob's ladder and onto the deck before the astonished yachtsmen realized that they were being boarded with sinister intent. At the same time, the Saigon struck the English flag and ran up the German.

Twenty-five or thirty men and a girl on the deck of the

31

yacht looked with amazement on the savage, piratical-appearing company confronting them with armed force.

"What is the meaning of this?" demanded the yacht's captain.

Schmidt pointed at the German flag flying above the Saigon. "It means that I am seizing you in the name of the German Government," replied Schmidt; "I am taking you over as a prize, and shall put a prize crew aboard. Your engineer and navigating officer will remain aboard. My first mate, Jabu Singh, will be in command. He has suffered a slight accident; your doctor will dress the wound, and the rest of you will return to my ship with me. You are to consider yourselves prisoners of war, and conduct yourselves accordingly."

"But, man," expostulated the Captain, "this vessel is not armed, it is not a warship, it is not even a merchant vessel; it is a private yacht on a scientific expedition. You, a merchantman, can't possibly contemplate taking us over."

"But I say, old thing!" said a tall young man in flannels; "you can't—"

"Shut up!" snapped Schmidt. "You are English, and that is enough reason for taking you over. Come now! Where's that doctor? Get busy."

While the doctor was dressing Jabu Singh's wound, Schmidt had his men search the ship for arms and ammunition. They found several pistols and sporting rifles; and, the doctor having finished with Jabu Singh, Schmidt detailed some of his men and left a few of the yacht's sailors to man the craft; then he herded the remainder into the Saigon's boat and returned with them to the steamer.

"I say," exclaimed the young man in white flannels, "this is a beastly outrage."

"It might have been worse, Algy," said the girl; "maybe you won't have to marry me now."

"Oh, I say, old thing," expostulated the young man; "this might even be worse."

# VI

The bullet that had dropped Tarzan had merely grazed his head, inflicting a superficial flesh wound and stunning him for a few minutes; but he had soon recovered and now he and Janette Laon watched the prisoners as they came over the side of the Saigon. "Schmidt has turned pirate," remarked the girl. "I wonder what he is going to do with all those people! There must be fifteen of them."

She did not have long to wait for an answer to her inquiry. Schmidt sent the eight crew members forward when they agreed to help man the Saigon; then he had two more iron cages hoisted to the deck and lined up with the two already there. "Now," he said, "I know I shouldn't do it, but I am going to let you choose your own cage mates."

"I say!" cried Algernon Wright-Smith; "you're not going to put the ladies in one of those things!"

"What's good enough for an English pig is good enough for an English sow," growled Schmidt; "hurry up and decide what you want to do."

An elderly man with a white walrus mustache, harrumphed angrily, his red face becoming purple. "You damned bounder!" he snorted; "you can't do a thing like that to English women."

"Don't excite yourself, Uncle," said the girl; "We'll have to do as the fellow says."

"I shall not step a foot into one of those things, William," said the second woman in the party, a lady who carried her fifty odd years rather heavily around her waist. "Nor shall Patricia," she added.

"Come come," expostulated the girl; "we're absolutely helpless, you know," and with that she entered the smaller of the two cages; and presently her uncle and her aunt, finally realizing the futility of resistance, joined her. Captain Bolton, Tibbet, the second mate of the yacht, Dr. Crouch, and Algy, were herded into the second cage.

Schmidt walked up and down in front of the cages, gloating. "A fine menagerie I am getting," he said; "A French girl, a German traitor, a Dutch dog, and seven English pigs: with my apes, monkeys, lions, tigers, and elephants we shall be a sensation in Berlin."

The cage in which the Leigh's and their niece were confined was next to that occupied by Tarzan and Janette Laon: and beyond the Leigh's cage was that in which the other four Englishmen were imprisoned.

Penelope Leigh eyed Tarzan askance and with aversion. "Shocking!" she whispered to her niece, Patricia; "the fellow is practically naked."

"He's rather nice looking, Aunty," suggested Patricia Leigh-Burdon.

"Don't look at him," snapped Penelope Leigh; "and that woman—do you suppose that is his wife?"

"She doesn't look like a wild woman," said Patricia.

"Then what is she doing alone in that cage with that man?" demanded Mrs. Leigh.

"Perhaps she was put there just the way. we were put here."

"Well!" snorted Penelope Leigh; "she looks like a loose woman to me."

"Now," shouted Schmidt, "we are about the feed the animals; everyone who is not on duty may come and watch."

Lascars, and Chinese, and several of the yacht's crew, gathered in front of the cages as food and water were brought; the former an unpalatable, nondescript mess, the contents of which it would have been difficult to determine, either by sight or taste. Tarzan was given a hunk of raw meat.

"Disgusting," snorting Penelope Leigh, as she pushed the unsavory mess from her. A moment later her attention was attracted by growls coming from the adjoining cage; and when she looked, she gasped, horror-stricken. "Look!" she whispered in a trembling voice; "that creature is growling, and he is eating his meat raw; how horrible!"

"I find him fascinating," said Patricia.

"Hurrumph!" growled Colonel William Cecil Hugh Percival Leigh; "filthy blighter."

"Canaille!" snapped Mrs. Leigh.

Tarzan looked up at Janette Laon, that shadowy smile just touching his lips, and winked.

"You understand English too?" she asked. Tarzan nodded. "Do you mind if I have some fun with them?" she continued.

"No," replied Tarzan; "go as far as you wish." They had both spoken in French and in whispers.

"Do you find the captain palatable," she asked in English loudly enough to be heard in the adjoining cage.

"He is not as good as the Swede they gave me last week," replied Tarzan.

Mrs. Leigh paled and became violently nauseated; she sat down suddenly and heavily. The colonel, inclined to be a little pop-eyed, was even more so as he gazed incredulously into the adjoining cage. His niece came close to him and whispered, "I think they are spoofing us, Uncle; I saw him wink at that girl."

"My smelling salts!" gasped Mrs. Leigh.

"What's the matter, colonel?" asked Algernon Wright-Smith, from the adjoining cage.

"That devil is eating the captain," replied the colonel in a whisper that could have been heard half a block away. De Groote grinned.

"My word!" exclaimed Algy. Janette Laon turned her head away to hide her laughter, and Tarzan continued to tear at the meat with his strong, white teeth.

"I tell you they are making fools of us," said Patricia Leigh-Burden. "You can't make me believe that civilized human beings would permit that man to eat human flesh, even if he wished to, which I doubt. When that girl turned away, I could see her shoulders shaking—she was laughing."

"What's that, William?" cried Mrs. Leigh, as the roar of a lion rose from the hold.

The animals had been unnaturally quiet for some time; but now they were getting hungry, and the complaint of the lion started them off, with the result that in a few moments of blood-curdling diapason of savagery billowed up from below: the rumbling roars of lions, the coughing growls of tigers, the hideous laughter of hyenas, the trumpeting of elephants mingled with the medley of sounds from the lesser beasts.

"Oh-h-h!" screamed Mrs. Leigh. "How hideous! Make them stop that noise at once, William."

"Harrumph!" said the colonel, but without his usual vigor. Presently, however, as the Chinese and Indian keepers fed the animals, the noise subsided and quiet was again restored.

As night approached, the sky became overcast and the wind increased, and with the rolling of the ship the animals again became restless. A Lascar came and passed buckets of water into all of the cages except that in which Tarzan was confined. To do this, he had to unlock the cage doors and raise them sufficiently to pass the pails through; then he passed in a broom, with which the inmates were supposed to clean their cages. Although he was accompanied by two other sailors armed with rifles, he did not unlock the door of Tarzan's cage, for Schmidt was afraid to take a chance on the wild man's escaping.

Tarzan had watched this procedure which had occurred daily ever since he had been brought aboard the Saigon. He knew that the same Lascar always brought the water and that he came again at about four bells of the first night watch to make a final inspection of the captives. On this tour of duty he came alone, as he did not have to unlock the cages; but Schmidt, in order to be on the safe side, had armed him with a pistol.

This afternoon, as he was passing the water into the cage occupied by the Leighs, the colonel questioned him. "Steward," he said, "fetch us four steamer chairs and rugs," and he handed the Lascar a five pound note.

The sailor took the note, looked at it, and stuffed it into his dirty loin cloth. "No chairs; no rugs," he said and started on toward the next cage.

"Hi, fellow!" shouted the colonel; "come back here! Who is captain of this ship? I want to see the captain."

"Sahib Schmidt captain now," replied the Lascar. "Captain Larsen sick; no see three, four days; maybe dead;" then he moved on and the colonel made no effort to detain him.

Mrs. Leigh shuddered. "It *was* the captain," she breathed in a horrified whisper, her terrified gaze rivetted on a bone in Tarzan's cage.

## VII

Rain fell in torrents and the wind whistled through the cages, driving it in myriad needle points against the unprotected inmates. The sea rose and the Saigon rolled and pitched heavily; lightning flashes illuminated the ship momentarily and heralded the deep booming of the following thunder which momentarily drowned out the roars and growls and trumpeting of terrified beasts.

Tarzan stood erect in his cage enjoying the lashing of the rain, the thunder, and the lightning. Each vivid flash revealed the occupants of adjoining cages, and during one of them he saw that the Englishman had placed his coat around the shoulders of his wife and was trying to shield her body from the storm with his own. The English girl stood erect, as did Tarzan, seeming to enjoy this battle with the elements. It was then that the ape man decided that he liked these two.

Tarzan was waiting; he was waiting for the Lascar to make his nightly inspection; but that night the Lascar did not come. The Lord of the Jungle could wait with that patience he had learned from the wild creatures among whom he had been reared; some night the Lascar would return.

The storm increased in fury; the Saigon was running before it now with great following seas always threatening to break over her stern. The wind howled in throaty anguish and hurled spume to join with the rain in deluging the miserable prisoners in their cages. Janette Laon lay down and tried to sleep. The English girl paced back and forth in the narrow confines of her cage. Tarzan watched her; he knew her type; an outdoor girl; the free swing of her walk proclaimed it. She would be efficient in anything she undertook, and she could endure hardship without complaining. Tarzan was sure of that, for he had watched her ever since she had been brought aboard the Saigon, had heard her speak, and had noticed her acceptance of the inevitable in a spirit similar to his own. He imagined that she would wait patiently until her opportunity came and that then she would act with courage and intelligence.

As he watched her now, taking the rain and the wind and the pitching of the ship as though they were quite the usual thing, she stopped at the side of her cage that adjoined his and looked at him.

"Did you enjoy the captain?" she asked with a quick smile.

"He was a little too salty," replied Tarzan.

"Perhaps the Swede was better," she suggested.

"Much; especially the dark meat."

"Why did you try to frighten us?" she asked.

"Your uncle and aunt were not very complimentary in their remarks about us."

"I know," she said. "I'm sorry, but they were very much upset. This has been a shocking experience for them. I am very much worried about them; they are old and cannot put up with much more of this. What do you think this man Schmidt intends doing with us?"

"There is no telling; the man is mad. His plan to exhibit us in Berlin is, of course, ridiculous. If he gets us to Berlin, we English will, of course, be interned."

"You are an Englishman?"

"My father and mother were English."

"My name is Burden—Patricia Leigh-Burden," said the girl; "may I ask yours?"

"Tarzan," replied the ape man.

"Just Tarzan?"

"That is all."

"Do you mind telling me how you happen to be in that cage, Mr. Tarzan?"

"Just Tarzan," he corrected her; "no mister. I happen to be in this cage because Abdullah Abu Néjm wished to be revenged; so he had me captured by an African chief who also had reason to wish to get rid of me. Abdullah sold me to a man by the name of Krause who was collecting animals to sell in America. Krause is in the cage next to mine on the other side. Schmidt, who was 2nd mate, has Krause's ship, his wild man, and all his animals. He also has Krause."

"He won't have any of us long if this storm gets much worse," said the girl. She was clinging to the bars of the

38

cage now, as the ship dove into the trough of a sea, rolling and wallowing as it was lifted to the crest of the next.

"The Saigon doesn't look like much," said Janette Laon, who had come to stand beside Tarzan, "but I think she will weather this storm all right. We ran into a worse one coming out. Of couse we had Captain Larsen in command then, nd Mr. de Groote was 1st mate; it may be a different story with Schmidt in command."

The ship swung suddenly, quartering to the sea, and slithered down into the trough, heeling over on her beam-ends. There was a frightened scream as a flash of lightning revealed the colonel and his wife being thrown heavily against the bars of their cage.

"Poor Aunt Penelope!" cried the English girl; "she can't stand much more of this." She worked her way around the side of the cage to her aunt. "Are you hurt, Auntie?" she asked.

"Every bone in my body is broken," said Mrs. Leigh. "I never did approve of that silly expedition. Who cares what lives at the bottom of the ocean, anyway—you'd never meet any of them in London. Now we have lost the Naiad and are about to lose our lives in the bargain. I hope your uncle is satisfied." Patricia breathed a sigh of relief, for she knew now that her aunt was all right. The Colonel maintained a discreet silence: twenty-five years experience had taught him when to keep still.

The long night passed, but the storm did not abate in fury. The Saigon still ran before it, slowed down to about five knots and taking it on her quarter. An occasional wave broke over the stern, flooding the decks, and almost submerging the inmates of the cages, who could only cling to the bars and hope for the best.

By her own testimony, Mrs. Leigh was drowned three times. "Hereafter, William," she said, "you should stick to *The Times,* Napoleon's campaigns, and Gibbon's Rome; the moment you read anything else you go quite off your head. If you hadn't read that Arcturus Adventure by that Beebe person, we would undoubtedly be safe at home in England this minute. Just because he fished up a lot of hideous crea-

39

tures equipped with electric lights, you had to come out and try it; I simply cannot understand it, William."

"Don't be too hard on Uncle," said Patricia; "he might have found some with hot and cold running water and become famous."

"Humph!" snorted Mrs. Leigh.

That day no one approached the cages, and neither food nor water was brought to the captives. The animals below deck fared similarly, and their plaints rose above the howling of the storm. It was not until late in the afternoon of the third day that two of the Chinese sailors brought food, and by this time the captives were so famished that they wolfed it ravenously, notwithstanding the fact that it was only a cold and soggy mess of ship's biscuit.

Mrs. Leigh had lapsed into total silence; and both her niece and her husband were worried, for they knew that when Penelope Leigh failed to complain there must be something radically wrong with her.

At about nine o'clock that night, the wind suddenly died down; the calm that ensued was ominous. "We have reached the center of it," said Janette Laon.

"Soon it will be bad again," said Tarzan.

"The fool should have run out of it, not into it," said Janette.

Tarzan was waiting patiently, like a lion at a waterhole—waiting for his prey to come. "It is better thus," he said to the girl.

"I do not understand," she replied, "I do not see how it could be worse."

"Wait," he said, "and I think you will see presently."

While the seas were still high, the Saigon seemed to be taking them better now, and presently Schmidt appeared on deck and came down to the cages. "How's the livestock?" he demanded.

"These women will die if you keep them in here, Schmidt," said de Groote. "Why can't you take them out and give them a cabin, or at least put them below decks where they will be protected from the storm?"

"If I hear any more complaints," said Schmidt, "I'll dump the whole lot of you overboard, cages and all. What do you want anyway? You're getting free transportation, free food, and private rooms. You've been getting free shower baths, too, for the last three days."

"But, man, my wife will die if she is exposed much longer," said Colonel Leigh.

"Let her die," said Schmidt, "I need some fresh meat for the wild man and the other animals," with which parting pleasantry, Schmidt returned to the bridge.

Mrs. Leigh was sobbing, and the Colonel was cursing luridly. Tarzan was waiting, and presently that for which he was waiting came to pass; Asoka, the Lascar, was coming to make his belated inspection. He swaggered a little, feeling the importance of being keeper of English sahibs and their ladies.

The ship's lights relieved the darkness sufficiently so that objects were discernible at some distance, and Tarzan, whose eyes were trained by habit to see at night, had recognized Asoka immediately he came on deck.

The ape-man stood grasping two adjacent bars of his cage as Asoka passed, keeping well out of arm's reach of the wild man. Janette Laon stood beside Tarzan; she intuitively sensed that something important was impending.

Her eyes were on her cage mate; she saw the muscles of his shoulders and his arms tense as he exerted all their tremendous power upon the bars of his cage. And then she saw those bars slowly spread and Tarzan of the Apes step through to freedom.

# VIII

Asoka, the Lascar, swaggered on past the cage of the Leigh's, and when he was opposite that in which the four Englishmen were confined, steel-thewed fingers closed upon his throat from behind, and his gun was snatched from its holster.

Janette Laon had watched with amazement the seeming ease with which those Herculean muscles had separated the bars. She had seen Tarzan overtake the Lascar and disarm him; and now she stepped through the opening after him, carrying the pistols they had taken from Schmidt and Jabu Singh.

Asoka struggled and tried to cry out until a grim voice whispered in his ear, "Quiet, or I kill;" then he subsided.

Tarzan glanced back and saw Janette Laon behind him. Then he took the key to the cages which hung about Asoka's neck on a piece of cord and handed it to the girl. "Come with me and unlock them," he said, and passed around the end of the last cage to the doors, which were on the opposite side.

"You men will come with me," said Tarzan in a whisper; "the Colonel and the women will remain here."

As Tarzan came opposite the cage of the Leigh's, Mrs. Leigh, who had been dozing during the lull in the storm, awoke and saw him. She voiced a little scream and cried, "The wild man has escaped!"

"Shut up, Penelope," growled the Colonel; "he is going to let us out of this damn cage."

"Don't you dare curse me, William Cecil Hugh Percival Leigh," cried Penelope.

"Quiet," growled Tarzan, and Penelope Leigh subsided into terrified silence.

"You may come out," said Tarzan, "but remain close to the cages until we return." Then he followed Janette to the cage in which de Groote and Krause were imprisoned and waited until she had removed the padlock.

"De Groote may come out," he said; "Krause will remain.

Asoka, you get in there." He turned to Janette. "Lock them in," he said. "Give me one of the pistols and keep the other yourself; if either of these two tries to raise an alarm, shoot him. Do you think you could do that?"

"I shot Jabu Singh," she reminded him.

Tarzan nodded and then turned to the men behind him; he handed Asoka's pistol to de Groote. He had appraised the other men since they had come aboard, and now he told Janette to give her second pistol to Tibbet, the second mate of the Naiad.

"What is your name?" he asked.

"Tibbet," replied the mate.

"You will come with me. We will take over on the bridge. De Groote knows the ship. He and the others will look for arms. In the meantime, pick up anything you can to fight with, for there may be fighting."

The ship had passed beyond the center of the storm, and the wind was howling with renewed violence. The Saigon was pitching and rolling violently as Tarzan and Tibbet ascended the ladder to the bridge, where the Lascar, Chand, was at the wheel and Schmidt on watch. By chance, Schmidt, happened to turn just as Tarzan entered, and seeing him, reached for his gun, at the same time shouting a warning to Chand. Tarzan sprang forward, swift as Ara, the lightning, and struck up Schmidt's hand just as he squeezed the trigger. The bullet lodged in the ceiling, and an instant later, Schmidt was disarmed. In the meantime, Tibbet had covered Chand and disarmed him.

"Take the wheel," said Tarzan, "and give me the other gun. Keep a look-out behind you and shoot anyone who tries to take over. You two get down to the cages," he said to Schmidt and Chand. He followed them down the ladder to the deck and herded them to the cage where Krause and Asoka were confined.

"Open that up, Janette," he said; "I have two more animals for our menagerie."

"This is mutiny," blustered Schmidt, "and when I get you to Berlin, you'll be beheaded for it."

"Get in there," said Tarzan, and pushed Schmidt so violently, that when he collided with Krause, both men went down.

Above the din of the storm they heard a shot from below, and Tarzan hurried in the direction from which the sound had come. As he descended the ladder, he heard two more shots and the voices of men cursing and screams of pain.

As he came upon the scene of the fight, he saw that his men had been taken from the rear by armed Lascars, but there seemed to have been more noise than damage. One of the Lascars had been wounded. It was he who was screaming. But aside from the single casualty, no damage seemed to have been done on either side. Three of the four Lascars remained on their feet, and they were firing wildly and indiscriminately, as Tarzan came up behind them carrying a gun in each hand.

"Drop your pistols," he said, "or I kill."

The three men swung around then, almost simultaneously. Looking into the muzzles of Tarzan's two pistols, two of the Lascars dropped theirs, but the third took deliberate aim and fired. Tarzan fired at the same instant, and the Lascar clutched at his chest and lurched forward upon his face.

The rest was easy. De Groote found the pistols, rifles, and ammunition taken from the Naiad in Schmidt's cabin, and with all the rest of the party disarmed, Oubanovitch and the remaining Lascars put up no resistance. The Chinese and the impressed members of the Naiad's crew had never offered any, being more than glad to be relieved of service under a madman.

The ship safely in his hands, Tarzan gathered his party into the ship's little saloon. Penelope Leigh still regarded him with disgust not unmixed with terror; to her he was still a wild man, a cannibal who had eaten the Captain and the Swede and would doubtless, sooner or later, eat all of them. The others, however, were appreciative of the strength and courage and intelligence which had released them from a dangerous situation.

"Bolton," said Tarzan to the captain of the Naiad, "you will take command of the ship; de Groote will be your first mate, Tibbet your second. De Groote tells me there are only two cabins on the Saigon. Colonel and Mrs. Leigh will take the Captain's cabin, the two girls will take that which was occupied by the mates."

"He is actually giving orders to us," Penelope Leigh whispered to her husband; "you should do something about it, William; you should be in command."

"Don't be silly, Auntie," snapped Patricia Leigh-Burden, in a whisper; "we owe everything to this man. He was magnificent. If you had seen him spread those bars as though they were made of lead!"

"I can't help it," said Mrs. Leigh; "I am not accustomed to being ordered about by naked wild men; why doesn't somebody loan him some trousers?"

"Come, come, Penelope," said the Colonel, "if you feel that way about it I'll loan him mine—haw!!—then I won't have any—haw! haw!"

"Don't be vulgar, William," snapped Mrs. Leigh.

Tarzan went to the bridge and explained to de Groote the arrangements that he had made. "I'm glad you didn't put me in command," said the Dutchman; "I haven't had enough experience. Bolton should be a good man. He used to be in the Royal Navy. How about Oubanovitch?"

"I have sent for him," replied Tarzan, "he should be here in a moment."

"He's against everybody," said de Groote, "a died-in-the-wool Communist. Here he comes now."

Oubanovitch slouched in, sullen and suspicious. "What are you two doing up here?" he demanded; "where's Schmidt?"

"He is where you are going if you don't want to carry on with us," replied Tarzan.

"Where's that?" asked Oubanovitch.

"In a cage with Krause and a couple of Lascars," replied the ape-man. "I don't know whether you had anything to do with the mutiny or not, Oubanovitch, but if you care to continue on as engineer, nobody is going to ask any questions."

The scowling Russian nodded. "All right," he said; "you can't be no worse than that crazy Schmidt."

"Captain Bolton is in command. Report to him and tell him that you are the engineer. Do you know what has become of the Arab? I haven't seen him for several days."

"He's always in the engine room keeping warm."

"Tell him to report to me here on the bridge and ask Captain Bolton to send us a couple of men."

The two men strained their eyes out into the darkness ahead. They saw the ship's nose plow into a great sea from which she staggered sluggishly. "It's getting worse," remarked de Groote.

"Can she weather much more?" asked Tarzan.

"I think so," said de Groote, "as long as I can keep it on her quarter, we can keep enough speed to give her steerageway."

A shot sounded from behind them, and the glass in the window in front of them shattered. Both men wheeled about to see Abdullah Abu Néjm standing at the top of the ladder with a smoking pistol in his hand.

## IX

The Arab fired again, but the plunging and the pitching of the Saigon spoiled his aim and he missed just as Tarzan sprang for him.

The impact of the ape-man's body carried Abdullah backward from the ladder, and both men crashed heavily to the deck below, the Arab beneath—a stunned, inert mass.

The two sailors, whom Captain Bolton was sending to the bridge, came on deck just in time to see what had happened; and they both ran forward, thinking to find a couple of broken, unconscious men, but there was only one in that condition.

Tarzan sprang to his feet, but Abdullah Abu Néjm lay where he had fallen. "One of you men go below and ask Miss Laon for the keys to the cages," Tarzan directed; then he seized the Arab by the arms and dragged him back to the cage in which Krause and Schmidt were confined, and when the key was brought, he opened the door and tossed the Arab in. Whether the man were alive or dead, Tarzan did not know or care.

The storm increased in fury, and shortly before daylight the steamer fell into the trough of the sea, rolling on its beam-ends and hanging there for an instant, as though about to capsize; then it would roll back the other way and for another harrowing moment the end seemed inevitable. The change in the motion of the ship awakened Tarzan instantly, and he made his way to the bridge—a feat that was not too difficult for a man who had been raised in a forest by apes and swung through the trees for the greater part of his life, for he climbed to the bridge more often than he walked. He found the two sailors clinging to the wheel, and the Captain to a stanchion.

"What's happened?" he asked.

"The rudder's carried away," said Bolton. "If we could rig a sea anchor, we might have a chance of riding it out; but that is impossible in this sea. How the devil did you get up here, with the ship standing on her beam-ends as fast as she can roll from one side to the other?"

"I climbed," said Tarzan.

Bolton grumbled something that sounded like, "most extraordinary;" then he said, "I think it's letting up; if she can take this, we ought to be able to pull through, though even then we're going to be in a pretty bad fix, as I understand from one of these men, that that fellow, Schmidt, destroyed the radio."

As though to prove what she could do or couldn't do, the Saigon rolled over until her decks were vertical—and hung there. "My God!" cried one of the sailors; "she's going over!"

But she didn't go over; she rolled back, but not so far this time. The wind was coming in fitful gusts now; the storm was very definitely dying out.

Just before dawn, the Captain said, "Listen, do you hear that?"

"Yes," said Tarzan, "I have been hearing it for some time."

"Do you know what it is?" asked Bolton.

"I do," replied the ape-man.

"Breakers," said Bolton; "that's all we need to finish us up completely."

Slowly and grudgingly dawn came, as though held back by the same malign genie that had directed the entire cruise of the ill-fated Saigon. And, to leeward, the men on the bridge saw a volcanic island, its mountains clothed in tropical foliage, their summits hidden in low-hanging clouds. The seas were breaking on a coral reef a quarter-mile off shore, and toward this reef the Saigon was drifting.

"There is an opening in that reef to the right there," said Bolton. "I think we could lower boats now and get most of the people ashore."

"You're the Captain," said Tarzan.

Bolton ordered all hands on deck, and the men to their boat stations, but a number of Lascars seized the first boat and started lowering it away. De Groote rushed forward with drawn pistol in an effort to stop them; but he was too late, as they had already lowered away. His first inclination

48

was to fire into them as an example to the others, but instead he turned and held off the remaining Lascars, who were about to seize a second boat. Bolton and Tibbet joined him with drawn pistols, and the Lascars fell back.

"Shoot the first man who disobeys an order," directed Bolton. "Now," he continued, "we'll wait to see how that boat fares before we lower another."

The Saigon was drifting helplessly toward the reef, as passengers and crew lined the rail watching the crew of the life-boat battling the great seas in an effort to make the opening in the reef.

"If they make it at all, it's going to be close," said Dr. Crouch.

"And the closer in the Saigon drifts, the more difficult it is going to be for following boats," said Colonel Leigh.

"The bounders will never make it," said Algy, "and serves them jolly well right."

"I believe they are going to make it," said Patricia. "What do you think, Tarzan?"

"I doubt it," replied the ape-man, "and if they can't make it with every oar manned and no passengers, the other boats wouldn't have a ghost of a show."

"But isn't it worth trying?" asked the girl. "If the Saigon goes on that reef, we are all lost; in the boat we would, at least, have a fighting chance."

"The wind and the sea are both going down," said Tarzan; "there is quiet water just beyond the reef, and as the Saigon wouldn't break up immediately, I think we would have a better chance that way than in the boats, which would be stove in and sunk the moment they struck the reef."

"I think you are right there," said Bolton; "but in an emergency like this, were all our lives are at stake, I can speak only for myself; I shall remain with the ship, but if there are enough who wish to take to a boat to man it properly, I will have number four boat lowered"; he looked around at the ship's company, but every eye was upon the boat driving toward the reef and no one seemed inclined to take the risk.

"They're not going to make it," said Tibbet.

"Not by a long way," agreed Dr. Crouch.

"Look!" exclaimed Janette Laon, "they're running straight for it now."

"The bounders have got more sense than I thought they had," growled Colonel Leigh; "they see they can't make the opening and now they are going to try to ride a wave over the reef."

"With luck they may make it," said Bolton.

"They'll need the luck of the Irish," said Crouch.

"There they go!" cried Algy. "Look at the bloody blighters row."

"They took that wave just right," said Tibbet; "they're riding it fast."

"There they go!" cried Janette.

The lifeboat was rushing toward the reef just below the crest of a great sea, the Lascars pulling furiously to hold their position. "They're over!" cried Patricia. But they were not; the prow struck a projecting piece of coral, and the on-rushing breaker upended the boat, hurling the Lascars into the lagoon.

"Well, the men got across if the boat didn't," remarked Crouch.

"I hope they can swim," said Janette.

"I hope they can't," growled the Colonel.

They watched the men floundering in the water for a minute or two as they started to swim toward shore, and then Janette exclaimed, "Why, they're standing up; they're walking!"

"That not surprising," said Bolton; "many of these coral lagoons are shallow."

Both the wind and the sea were dying down rapidly, and the Saigon was drifting, but slowly, toward the reef; however, it would not be long before she struck. The Saigon, illy equipped, afforded only a few life belts. Three of these were given to the women, and the others to members of the crew who said they could not swim.

"What do you think our chances are, Captain?" asked Colonel Leigh.

"If we are lifted on the reef, we may have a chance, if she hangs there for even a few minutes," replied Bolton, "but if she's stove in before she lodges, she'll sink in deep water on this side of the reef, and—well—you're guess is as good as mine, sir; I'm going to have the rafts unshipped, the boats lowered on deck and out loose—get as much stuff loose as will float and carry people," and he gave orders to the crew to carry out this work.

While the men were engaged in this work, there came a shout from amidships: "Hi there, de Groote!" called Krause; "are you going to leave us here to drown like rats in a trap?"

De Groote looked at Tarzan questioningly, and the ape-man turned to Janette. "Let me have the key to the cages," he said, and when she had handed it to him, he went to the cage in which Krause and the others were confined. "I'm going to let you out," he said, "but see that you behave yourselves; I have plenty of reason to kill all of you white men, and I won't need much more of an excuse."

Abdullah was a sick-looking Arab, and all three of the white men were sullen and scowling as they came out of the cage.

As they approached the rail, Bolton shouted, "Stand by the boats and rafts; she's going to strike!"

# X

The ship's company stood in tense expectancy as a wave lifted the Saigon above a maelstrom of water surging over the reef.

As the sea dropped them with terrific impact upon the jagged coral rocks, the grinding and splintering of wood sounded her death knell. She reeled drunkenly toward the deep water outside the reef. More than one heart stood still in that tense moment; if she slipped back into the sea many would be lost, and there was no doubt now but that she was slipping.

"Percy," said Mrs. Leigh to the Colonel—she always called him Percy in her softer moods—"Percy, if I have been trying at times, I hope that you will forgive me now that we face our Maker."

"Harrumph!" grunted the Colonel. "It is all my fault; I should never have read that Beebe yarn."

As the Saigon slipped back into deep water, a following wave, larger than that which had preceded it, lifted the ship again and dropped her heavily upon the reef. This time she lodged firmly, and as the wave receded, she was left resting with her decks almost level.

"I say," said Algy, "this is a little bit of all right, what? Just like Noah's Ark—a bally old tub full of wild animals sitting high and dry on top of Mount Ararat."

A succession of smaller waves beat against the Saigon while the men worked to get the boats and the rafts over into the lagoon; and then another large wave broke entirely over the ship, but she did not budge from her position.

Lines leading to the ship held the boats and the rafts from drifting away, but now the question arose as to how to get the women down to them. The reef was narrow, and the Saigon rested only a few feet from its shoreward side. An athletic man might leap from the rail, clear the reef, and land in the lagoon; but Mrs. Leigh was not an athletic man, and she was the real problem.

She looked down over the rail of the ship at the waters still surging across the reef. "I can never get down there, William," she said; "you go on. Pay no attention to me; perhaps we shall meet in a happier world."

"Bosh and nonsense!" exclaimed the Colonel. "We'll get you down someway."

"I'll go down there," said Tarzan, "and you lower her from one of the ship's davits; I'll see that she's gotten on one of the rafts safely."

"Never," said Mrs. Leigh emphatically.

Tarzan turned to Captain Bolton. "I shall expect you to lower her immediately," he said, "and there will be no nonsense about it. I'm going down now to see how deep the water is inside the reef. Those who can't swim can jump in, and I will help them into one of the boats or onto a raft." He climbed to the top of the rail, poised there a moment, and then leaped far out, and dove towards the lagoon.

All hands started towards the rail to watch him. They saw him make a shallow dive and then turn over and disappear beneath the surface. Presently his head broke the water, and he looked up. "It is plenty deep right here," he said.

Patricia Leigh-Burden stripped off her life belt, climbed to the rail, and dove. When she came up, Tarzan was beside her. "I don't need to ask if you can swim," he said.

She smiled. "I'll stay here and help you with the others," she said.

Janette Laon was the next to jump. She did not dive, and she just cleared the reef.

Tarzan had hold of her before she reached the surface. He still supported her when their heads were above water.

"Can you swim?" he asked.

"No," she replied.

"You are a very brave girl," he said, as he swam towards one of the boats with her and helped her aboard.

By this time, they had rigged a boatswain's chair and were lowering a highly irate and protesting Mrs. Leigh over the ship's side. As she reached the surface of the lagoon, Tarzan was awaiting her.

"Young man," she snapped, "If anything happens to me, it will be your fault."

"Be quiet," said Tarzan, "and get out of that chair."

Probably in all her life, Penelope Leigh had never before been spoken to in the voice of real authority; it not only took her breath away, but it cowed her; and she slipped meekly out of the boatswain's chair and into Tarzan's arms. He swam with her to one of the rafts and helped her on, for they were easier to board than the lifeboats.

Tarzan swam back to the ship. The boatswain's chair was still swinging close above the water. He seized it and climbed hand over hand to the deck. One by one, men were jumping or diving from the rail when he stopped them.

"I want ten or fifteen volunteers for some very dangerous work," he said; "they have got to have what the Americans call 'guts'."

"What do you intend doing," asked Bolton.

"Now that everybody else is safely on shore, I am going to set the animals free," said the ape man, "and make them take to the water."

"But, man," cried Colonel Leigh, "many of them are dangerous beasts of prey."

"Their lives are as important to them as ours are to us," replied Tarzan, "and I am not going to leave them here to die of starvation."

"Quite right, quite right," said the Colonel, "but why not destroy them. That would be the humane way."

"I did not suggest destroying your wife or your friends," said Tarzan, "and nobody is going to destroy my friends."

"Your friends?" ejaculated the Colonel.

"Yes, my friends," replied the Lord of the Jungle, "or perhaps it would be better to say, my people. I was born and raised among them; I never saw a human being until I was almost grown, nor did I see a white man 'til I was fully twenty years old. Will anyone volunteer to help me save them?"

"By Jove!" exclaimed the Colonel; "that is certainly a sporting proposition; I'm with you, young man."

De Groote, Bolton, Tibbet, Crouch, a number of the Naiad crew and several Chinese volunteered to help him, as well as the three Indian keepers, who had been signed on by Krause to look after the animals.

While those who had not volunteered to remain with him were leaving the ship, Tarzan released the Orang-utans. He spoke to them in their own language, and they clung to him like frightened children; then he led his men below to the animal deck and opened the great double doors in the side of the ship, through which all of the larger animals had been loaded.

There were three Indian elephants, and these he liberated first, as they were docile and well trained. He had one of the Indian mahouts mount the best of these and told him to ride this one into the lagoon the moment that a wave covered the reef. There was a brief battle with the animal before it could be forced to take the plunge; but once he was swimming, it was comparatively easy to get the other two elephants to follow him, and then the African elephants were released. These were wild beasts and far more dangerous and difficult, but once their leader saw the Indian elephants swimming away he lumbered into the lagoon and followed, and his fellows trailed after him.

The cages of the lions and tigers were dragged one by one to the door, the doors of the cages opened, and the cages tilted until the beasts were spilled out. The lesser animals were disembarked in the same way.

It was a long and arduous job, but at last it was over, and only the snakes remained.

"What are you going to do about them?" asked Bolton.

"Histah, the snake, has always been my enemy," replied Tarzan; "him, we shall destroy."

They stood in the doorway of the ship watching the beasts making their way toward shore, from which the empty boats and rafts were already being returned to the ship in accordance with Bolton's orders.

Along the shore line was a narrow beach, and beyond that dense jungle broke gradually upward to the foot of the green-clad, volcanic mountains which formed a fitting backdrop for the wild and desolate scene.

The landing party huddled on the beach as the wild creatures swam or waded to shore. But the animals bolted into the jungle as fast as they came out of the water. A single elephant turned and trumpeted, and a lion roared, whether in challenge or thanksgiving, who may know? And then the jungle closed about them, and they took up their new lives in a strange world.

Most of the sailors had returned to the ship with the rafts and boats, and the remainder of the day was spent in transporting the ship's stores to the beach.

For two days they worked, stripping the ship of everything that might add to their comfort or convenience, and while half of the men worked at this, the other half cut a clearing in the jungle, for a permanent camp. They had chosen this site because a little stream of fresh water ran through it.

In the afternoon of the third day when the work was almost completed, a little party of a dozen men looked down upon the camp from the summit of the cliff that hemmed the beach upon the south. Concealed by the verdure there, they watched the first strangers who had come to their island for many a long year.

## XI

The men who watched the castaways of the Saigon were warriors. They wore waist girdles which passed between their legs; the ends which hung down from the back, were elaborately embroidered with colored threads or feather mosaic work; over their shoulders was draped a square mantle, and they wore sandals made of hide. Their heads were adorned with feather headdresses, and one among them wore one of feather mosaic; his dress ornaments were of jade, and his belt and sandals were studded with jade and gold, as were his armlets and leglets; in his nose was a carved ornament, which passed through a hole in the septum; his lip and earplugs were likewise of jade. All the trappings of this man were more gorgeous than those of his companions, for Xatl Din was a noble.

The brown faces of all were tattooed, but the tattooing on Xatl Din was by far the most elaborate. They were armed with bows and arrows, and each carried two quivers; each also carried a spear, and a sling to hurl stones. In addition to these weapons, each of the warriors carried a long sword made of hard wood, into the sides of which were set at intervals blades of obsidian. For protection, they carried wooden shields covered with the skins of animals. They watched the strangers for some time and then melted away into the jungle behind them.

The ship's charts and instruments had been brought ashore, and that noon Captain Bolton had sought to establish their position; but when he had done so and had consulted the chart, he discovered that there was no land within hundreds of miles in any direction.

"There must have been something wrong with my calculations," he said to de Groote; so they checked and double-checked, but the result was always the same—they were somewhere in the middle of the south Pacific, hundreds of miles from land.

"It can't be possible," said Bolton, "that there is an undiscovered and uncharted island anywhere in the world."

"I should have said as much," agreed de Groote, "until now; your figures are absolutely correct, sir, and we are on an uncharted island."

"With about as much chance of ever being picked up," said Bolton, "as we would be if we were on the moon. If no ship has touched here since the days of da Gama, it is safe to assume that no ship will touch here during the rest of our lifetime."

"If no ship has touched here in four hundred years," said de Groote, "our chances are really excellent, for there has got to be a first time you know; and the law of chance, that this island will remain undiscovered, is just about run out."

"You mean the statutes of limitations will operate in our favor," laughed Bolton. "Well, I hope you're right."

Tarzan had worked with the others. Comfortable shelters had been erected for the Colonel and his wife and for the two girls.

Now Tarzan summoned the entire company. "I have called you together," he said, "to say that we will form two camps. I will not have Abdullah, Krause, Schmidt, Oubanovitch, or the Lascars in this camp. They have caused all the trouble. Because of them we are castaways on an uncharted island, where, according to Captain Bolton, we may have to spend the rest of our lives. If we permit them to remain in our camp, they will again make trouble; I know the kind of men they are," then he turned to Krause. "You will take your party north, at least two long marches, and don't any of you come within ten miles of this camp. If you do, I kill. That is all. Go."

"We'll go, all right," said Oubanovitch, "but we'll take our share of the provisions, firearms, and amunition."

"You will take your lives, and that is all," said Tarzan.

"You don't mean that you're going to send them away into this strange jungle without food or weapons," demanded the Colonel.

"That is exactly what I mean," said Tarzan, "and they are lucky that it is no worse."

"You can't do that to us," shouted Oubanovitch, "you can't keep a lot of dirty Capitalists in affluence and grind down the poor working man. I know your type, a fawning sycophant, hoping to curry favor with the rich and powerful."

"My word!" exclaimed Algy, "the blighter's making a speech."

"Just like Hyde Park," said Patricia.

"That's right," screamed Oubanovitch; "the smart bourgeosie ridiculing the honest laboring man."

"Get out," growled Tarzan.

Abdullah pulled at Oubanovitch's sleeve. "You'd better come," he whispered; "I know that fellow; he is a devil; he would rather kill us than not."

The others started moving away towards the north, and they dragged Oubanovich along with them; but he turned and shouted back, "I'll go, but I'll be back, when the poor slaves that are working for you now realize that they should be the masters, not you."

"Well!" exclaimed Penelope Leigh, "I'm glad that they are gone; that is something, at least," and she cast a meaningful glance at Tarzan.

Coconut palms and bananas grew in profusion in the jungle around the camp, and there were breadfruit and edible tubers and a few papaya trees, while the lagoon abounded in fish; so there was little likelihood of their starving, but Tarzan craved flesh.

After the camp was completed, he set to work to make the weapons of the chase which he liked best to use. His bow, arrows, and quiver, he had to make himself; but among the ships stores, he found a suitable knife and a rope and, from a gaff, he fashioned a spear. This last was a tacit acknowledgment of the presence of the great carnivores he had turned loose upon the island. And then, one morning, Tarzan disappeared from camp before the others had awakened. He followed the course of the little stream that ran down from the verdure-clad hills, but, to avoid the tangle of underbrush, he swung through the trees.

I said that he had left camp before the others were awake; and this was what Tarzan thought, but presently he sensed that he was being followed and looking back, saw the two orang-utans swinging through the trees in his wake.

"Tarzan hunts," he said in the language of the great apes, when they had come up to him; "make no noise."

"Tarzan hunts, mangani make no noise," one of them assured him. And so the three of them swung silently through the trees of the silent forest.

On the lower slopes of the mountains, Tarzan came upon the elephants eating on tender shoots. He spoke to them, and they rumbled a greeting in their throats. They were not afraid, and they did not move away. Tarzan thought he would learn how friendly they might be, and so he dropped down close beside a great African bull and spoke to him in the language that he had used all his life when conversing with his beloved Tantor.

It is not really a language, and I do not know what name to call it by, but through it Tarzan could convey his feelings more than his wishes to the great beasts that had been his playfellows since his childhood.

"Tantor," he said, and laid his hand upon the great beast's shoulder. The huge bull swayed to and fro and reached back and touched the ape-man with his trunk, an inquisitive, questioning touch; and, as Tarzan spoke soothingly, the touch became a caress. And then the ape-man moved around in front of the great beast and laid his hand upon his trunk and said, "Nala!" The trunk moved smoothly over his body, and Tarzan repeated, "Nala! Tantor, Nala!"; and then the trunk wound around him and lifted him in air.

"B'yat, Tantor," commanded Tarzan, "tand b'yat!" and the bull lowered Tarzan to his head.

"Vando!" said Tarzan, and scratched the great beast behind his ears.

The other elephants went on with their feeding, paying no further attention to the ape-man, but the orang-utans sat in a nearby tree and scolded, for they were afraid of Tantor.

Now, Tarzan thought that he would try an experiment, and he swung from the bull's back into a nearby tree and went off a little distance into the jungle; then he called back, "yud, Tantor, yud b'yat."

Through the forest and the undergrowth came an answering rumble from the throat of the bull. Tarzan listened; he heard the cracking of twigs and the crashing of underbrush, and presently the great bulk of Tantor loomed above him.

"Vando, Tantor," he said, and swung away through the trees, much to the relief of the orang-utans, who had looked with disfavor upon this whole procedure.

The mountain rose steeply before them now, and there were often places where only Tarzan or his simian friends might go. At last the three came to a ledge that ran towards the south. It led away from the stream, however, from which Tarzan had departed at the foot of a waterfall which tumbled over a cliff the precipitous and slippery sides of which might have been negotiated by a fly or a lizard but by little else.

They followed the ledge around a shoulder of the mountain and came out upon a large level mesa dense with forest. It looked to Tarzan like a good hunting ground, and here he again took to the trees.

Presently, Usha, the wind, brought to his nostrils a familiar scent—the scent of Horta, the boar. Here was meat, and instantly Tarzan was the wild beast stalking its prey.

He had not gone far, however, before two other scents impinged upon his sensitive nostrils—the scent spoor of Numa, the lion, and mingled with it, that of man.

These two scent spoors could be mingled for but one of two reasons; either the man was hunting the lion, or the lion was hunting the man. And as Tarzan detected the scent of only a single man, he assumed that the lion was the hunter, and so he swung off through the trees, in the direction from which the scent came.

## XII

Thak Chan was hunting no lion. It was impossible that he could have been hunting a lion, for he had never seen or heard of one in all his life; neither had any of his progenitors through all recorded time. A long time ago, before Chac Tutul Xiu had migrated from Yucatan, Thak Chan's people had known the jaguar, and the memory of it had been carried across the great water to this distant island and preserved in enduring stone in the temples and upon the stelae that had been built here. Thak Chan was a hunter from the city of Chichen Itza, that Chac Tutul Xiu had founded upon this island which he had found and had named Uxal for the city of his birth.

Thak Chan was hunting the wild boar, which, if aroused, may be quite as formidable as Numa, the lion; but, up to now, Thak Chan had had no luck.

Thak Chan entered a small natural clearing in the forest, and as he did so, his startled attention was attracted to the opposite side by an ominous growl. Confronting him was the snarling face of the most terrifying beast he had ever seen.

The great lion slunk slowly out into the clearing, and Thak Chan turned and fled. The thunderous roar that followed him almost paralyzed him with terror as he raced for his life through the familiar mazes of the forest, while close behind the hungry lion loped after its prey. There could have been no hope for Thak Chan in that unequal race even if he had remained upon his feet; but when he tripped and fell, he knew that it was the end. He turned to face this fearsome, unknown creature; but he did not arise, and, still sitting on the ground, he awaited the attack with poised spear.

The lion appeared then from around a curve in the jungle trail. His yellow-green eyes were round and staring. To Thak Chan, they seemed burning with fires of fury. The beast's great yellow fangs were bared in a snarl so malignant, that

Thak Chan quailed anew. The lion did not charge; he merely trotted towards his prey, for here was only a puny man-thing—no worthy antagonist for the King of Beasts.

Thak Chan prayed to strange gods as he saw death approaching; and then, as though in answer to his prayers, an amazing thing happened; a naked man, a giant to Thak Chan, dove from a tree above the trail full upon the back of that savage beast for which Thak Chan did not even have a name. A mighty arm went around the beast's neck, and powerful legs wrapped around the small of its body. It rose upon its hind legs roaring hideously, and sought to reach the thing upon its back with fang or talon. It leaped into the air, twisting and turning; it threw itself upon the ground and rolled over in frantic effort to free itself: but the silent creature clung to it tenaciously, and with its free hand, drove a long knife again and again into its tawny side, until, with a final thunderous roar, the beast rolled over upon its side, quivered convulsively for a moment and lay still.

Thak Chan had watched this amazing battle with feelings of mixed terror and hope, half convinced that this was indeed a god come to save him, but almost as fearful of the god as of the beast.

As the great beast died, Thak Chan saw the man, or god, or whatever it was, rise to his feet and place one of them upon the body of his kill and then raise his face to the heavens and voice a long drawn out scream so terrifying that Thak Chan shuddered and covered his ears with his palms.

For the first time since it had risen from the floor of the ocean the island of Uxmal heard the victory cry of a bull ape that had made its kill.

# XIII

Thak Chan knew of many gods, and he tried to place this one. He knew them as the mighty ones, the captains that go before, and the old ones. There was Huitz-Hok, Lord Hills and Valleys; Che, Lord Forest; and innumerable earth gods; then of course there was Itzamna, ruler of the sky, son of Hunab Kuh, the first god and Hun Ahau, god of the underworld, Metnal, a cold, dank, gloomy place beneath the earth, where the rank and file and those who led evil lives went after death; and there was also Aychuykak, god of war, who was always carried into battle by four captains on a special litter.

Perhaps this one was Che, Lord Forest; and so Thak Chan addressed him thus, and being polite, thanked him for saving him from the strange beast. However, when Che replied, it was in a language that Thak Chan had never heard before, and which he thought perhaps was the language of the gods.

Tarzan looked at the strange little brown man who spoke this amazing language which he could not understand; then he said, "Dako-zan," which in the language of the great apes means "meat;" but Thak Chan only shook his head and apologized for being so stupid.

Seeing that he was getting nowhere this way, Tarzan took an arrow from his quiver and with its point drew a picture of Horta, the boar, in the well-packed earth of the trail; then he fitted the arrow to his bow and drove the shaft into the picture behind the left shoulder.

Thak Chan grinned and nodded excitedly; then he motioned Tarzan to follow him. As he started away along the trail, he chanced to look up and see the two orang-utans perched above him and looking down at him. This was too much for the simple mind of Thak Chan; first the strange and horrible beast, then a god, and now these two hideous creatures. Trembling, Thak Chan fitted an arrow to his bow; but when he aimed it at the apes, Tarzan snatched the weapon from him, and called to the orang-utans, which came down and stood beside him.

Thak Chan was now convinced that these also were gods, and he was quite overcome by the thought that he was consorting with three of them. He wanted to hurry right back to Chichen Itza and tell everybody he knew of the miraculous happenings of this day, but then it occurred to him that nobody would believe him and that the priests might become angry. He recalled, too, that men had been chosen as victims of the sacrificial rites at the temple for for much less than this.

There must be some way. Thak Chan thought and thought as he led Tarzan of the Apes through the forest in search of wild boar; and at last he hit upon a magnificent scheme; he would lead the three gods back to Chichen Itza that all men might see for themselves that Thak Chan spoke the truth.

Tarzan thought that he was being led in search of Horta, the boar; and when a turn in the trail brought them to the edge of the jungle, and he saw an amazing city, he was quite as surprised as Thak Chan had been when he had come to the realization that his three companions were gods. Tarzan could see that the central part of the city was built upon a knoll on the summit of which rose a pyramid surmounted by what appeared to be a temple. The pyramid was built of blocks of lava which formed steep steps leading to the summit. Around the pyramid were other buildings which hid its base from Tarzan's view; and around all this central portion of the city was a wall, pierced occasionally by gates. Outside the wall were flimsy dwellings of thatch, doubtless the quarters of the poorer inhabitants of the city.

"Chichen Itza," said Thak Chan, pointing and beckoning Tarzan to follow him.

With the natural suspicion of the wild beast which was almost inherent with him, the ape man hesitated. He did not like cities, and he was always suspicious of strangers, but presently curiosity got the better of his judgment, and he followed Thak Chan toward the city. They passed men and women working in fields where maize, and beans, and tubers were being cultivated—a monument to the perspicacity of Chac Tutul Xiu, who over four hundred years before, had had the foresight to bring seeds and bulbs with him from Yucatan.

The men and women in the fields looked up in amazement as they saw Thak Chan's companions, but they were still more amazed when Thak Chan announced proudly that they were Che, Lord Forest, and two of the earth gods.

By this time, however, the nerves of the two earth gods had endured all that they could; and these deities turned and scampered off toward the jungle, lumbering along in the half stooping posture of the great apes. Thak Chan called after them pleadingly, but to no avail, and a moment later he watched them swing into the trees and disappear.

By this time, the warriors guarding the gates they were approaching had become very much interested and not a little excited. They had summoned an officer, and he was awaiting Thak Chan and his companion when they arrived before the gate. The officer was Xatl Din, who had commanded the party of warriors that had discovered the castaways upon the beach.

"Who are you," he demanded, "and whom do you bring to Chichen Itza?"

"I am Thak Chan, the hunter," replied Tarzan's companion, "and this is Che, Lord Forest, who saved me from a terrible beast that was about to devour me. The two who ran away were earth gods. The people of Chichen Itza must have offended them or they would have come into the city."

Xatl Din had never seen a god, but he realized that there was something impressive about this almost naked stranger who towered high above him and his fellows, for Tarzan's height was accentuated by the fact that the Maya are a small people; and compared with them, he looked every inch a god. However, Xatl Din was not wholly convinced, for he had seen strangers on the beach, and he guessed that this might be one of them.

"Who are you who comes to Chichen Itza?" he demanded of Tarzan. "If you are indeed Che, Lord Forest, give me some proof of it, that Cit Coh Xiu, the king, and Chal Yip Xiu, the ah kin mai, may prepare to welcome you befittingly."

"Che, Lord Forest, does not understand our language,

most noble one," interposed Thak Chan; "he understands only the language of the gods."

"The gods can understand all languages," said Xatl Din.

. "I should have said that he would not debase himself by speaking it," Thak Chan corrected himself. "Undoubtedly he understands all that we say, but it would not be meet for a god to speak the language of mortals."

"You know a great deal for a simple hunter," said Xatl Din superciliously.

"Those whom the gods make friends with must be very wise," said Thak Chan loftily.

Thak Chan had been feeling more and more important all along. Never before had he had such a protracted conversation with a noble, in fact he had seldom ever said more than, "Yes, most noble one," or "No, most noble one." Thak Chan's assurance and the impressive appearance of the stranger were, at last, too much for Xatl Din, and he admitted them into the city, accompanying them himself toward the temple which was a part of the king's palace.

Here were warriors and priests and nobles resplendent in feathers and jade; and to one of the nobles who was also a priest, Xatl Din repeated the story that Thak Chan had told him.

Tarzan, finding himself surrounded by armed men, again became suspicious, questioning the wisdom of his entry into this city which might prove a trap from which he might find it difficult to escape.

A noble had gone to inform Chal Yip Xiu, the high priest, that one who claimed to be Che, Lord Forest, had come to visit him in his temple.

Like most high priests, Chal Yip Xiu was a trifle skeptical about the existence of gods; they were all right for the common people, but a high priest had no need for them. As a matter of fact, he considered himself as a personification of all the gods, and his power in Chichen Itza lent color to this belief.

"Go fetch the hunter and his companion," he said to the noble who had brought the message.

Shortly thereafter, Tarzan of the Apes strode into the presence of Chal Yip Xiu, the high priest of Chichen Itza, and with him were Thak Chan, the hunter, and Xatl Din, the noble, with several of his fellows, and a score of warriors and lesser priests.

When Chal Yip Xiu saw the stranger, he was impressed; and, to be on the safe side, he addressed him respectfully; but when Xatl Din told him that the god refused to speak the language of mortals, the high priest became suspicious.

"You reported the presence of strangers on the beach," he said to Xatl Din; "could not this be one of them?"

"It could, holy one," replied the noble.

"If this one is a god," said Chal Yip Xiu, "then the others must all be gods. But you told me that their ship was wrecked and that they were cast ashore."

"That is right, holy one," replied Xatl Din.

"Then they are only mortals," said the high priest, "for gods would have controlled the winds and the waves, and their ship would not have been wrecked."

"That, too, is true, most wise one," agreed Xatl Din.

"Then this man is no god," stated Chal Yip Xiu, "but he will make an excellent sacrifice to the true gods. Take him away."

# XIV

At this unlooked for turn of affairs, Thak Chan was so shocked and astounded that, although he was only a poor hunter, he dared raise his voice in protest to Chal Yip Xiu, the ah kin mai. "But, most holy one," he cried, "you should have seen the things that he did. You should have seen the great beast which was about to devour me, and how he leaped upon its back and killed it; none but a god could have done such a thing. Had you seen all this and the two earth gods that accompanied him, you would know that he must indeed be Che, Lord Forest."

"Who are you?" demanded Chal Yip Xiu in a terrible voice.

"I am Thak Chan, the hunter," replied the now frightened man meekly.

"Then stick to your hunting, Thak Chan," warned Chal Yip Xiu, "or you will end upon the sacrificial block or in the waters of the sacred well. Get you gone." Thak Chan went; he sneaked out like a dog with its tail between its legs.

But when warriors laid hands upon Tarzan, that was a different story. Although he had not understood Chal Yip Xiu's words, he had known by the man's tone and demeanor that all was not well, and when he had seen Thak Chan sneak away, he was doubly convinced of it; and then warriors closed in and laid hands upon him.

The high priest had received him in a colonnade upon one side of a peristyle, and Tarzan's keen eyes had quickly taken in the entire scene immediately after he was ushered into the presence of the high priest. He had seen the garden behind the row of columns and the low buildings beyond the peristyle. What lay immediately beyond these buildings he did not know, but he did know that the city wall was not far away, and beyond the wall and the fields there was the forest.

He shook off the detaining hands of the warriors and leaped to the low platform where Chal Yip Xiu sat; and, hurling the high priest aside, he leaped into the garden, crossed the peristyle at a run and swarmed up the wall of the building beyond.

Warriors pursued him across the peristyle with imprecations and arrows and stones from the slings they carried; but only the imprecations reached him, and they were harmless.

He crossed the roof of the building and dropped into a street beyond. There were people in the street, but they fell back in terror as this bronze giant brushed them aside and trotted on toward the city wall. At the end of this street was a gate, but it was not the gate through which he had entered the city, and the warriors stationed here knew nothing of him; to them he was only an almost naked stranger, evidently a man of an alien race, and thus an enemy who had no business within the walls of Chichen Itza; so they tried to bar his way and arrest him, but Tarzan seized one of them and holding him by the ankles used him as a club to force his way through the other warriors and out of the gate.

He was free at last, but then he had never had any doubt but what he would be free, for he looked with contempt upon these little men, primitively armed. How could they hope to hold Tarzan, Lord of the Jungle. Just then a stone from one of their slings struck him on the back of the head; and he fell forward upon his face, unconscious.

When Tarzan regained consciousness, he found himself in a wooden cage in a room dimly lit by a single window. The walls of the room were of beautifully dressed and fitted blocks of lava. The window was about two feet square and was near the ceiling; there was also a doorway in the room, closed by a heavy wooden door, which Tarzan guessed was bolted upon the outside. He did not know what fate lay in store for him, but he imagined that it would be most unpleasant, for the face of Chal Yip Xiù had been cruel indeed, as had the faces of many of the priests and nobles.

Tarzan tested the bars of his wooden cage and smiled. He knew that he could walk out of that whenever he pleased but getting out of the room might be another question; the window would have been large enough had there not been two stone bars set in the opening; the door looked very substantial.

The back wall of the cage was about two feet from the back wall of the room. Upon this side, Tarzan ripped off two of the bars and stepped out of the cage. He went at once to the door but could neither open it nor force it; however, he waited patiently before it with one of the broken bars of his cage in his hand—he knew that someone would open that door eventually.

He did not know that he had been unconscious a long time and that night had passed and that it was day again. Presently he heard voices outside his cell; they grew in numbers and volume until he knew that there was a great concourse of people there, and now he heard the booming of drums and the throaty blasts of trumpets and the sound of chanting.

As he was wondering what was going on outside in the city, he heard the scraping of the bolt outside his door. He waited, the broken bar held firmly in one hand; and then the door opened and a warrior entered—a warrior to whom death came quickly and painlessly.

Tarzan stepped into the doorway and looked out. Almost directly in front of him, a priest stood in front of an altar across which a girl was stretched upon her back; four men in long embroidered robes and feather headdresses held her there, one at each leg and one at each arm. The priest stood above her with knife of obsidian raised above her breast.

Tarzan took in the whole picture at a glance. The girl meant nothing to him; the death of a human being did not mean much to him, he who had seen so many creatures die, and knew that death was the natural consequence of life; but the cruelty and heartlessness of the ceremony angered him, and he was imbued with a sudden desire to thwart the authors of it, rather than with any humanitarian urge to rescue the girl. The priest's back was toward him as he leaped from his cell and snatched the knife from the upraised hand; then he lifted the priest and hurled him against two of the lesser priests who held the girl, breaking their holds and sending them crashing to the temple floor. The other two

71

priests he struck down with his wooden club. The astounding performance left the onlookers stunned and breathless, and no hand was raised to stop him as he lifted the girl from the altar, slung her across one shoulder, and leaped through the temple doorway.

Tarzan recalled the route by which he had been brought to the palace temple, and he followed it back now out into the city, past two astounded guards at the palace gate. They saw him disappear into a side street; but they dared not desert their posts to follow him, but almost immediately a howling mob surged past them in pursuit of the stranger who had defiled their temple and snatched a sacrifice from the altar of their god.

The city was practically deserted, for all the inhabitants had gathered in the temple square to witness the sacrifice, and so Tarzan ran unmolested and unobserved through the narrow, winding side street of Chichen Itza. He ran swiftly, for he could hear the howls of the pursuing mob, and he had no wish to be overtaken by it.

The girl across his shoulder did not struggle to escape; she was far too terrified. Snatched from death by this strange almost naked giant, she could only apprehend what a terrible fate awaited her. She had heard the story that Thak Chan had told, for it had spread throughout the city; and she thought that perhaps this was indeed Che, Lord Forest. The vaguest hint of such a possibility would have so terrified little Itzl Cha that she could not have moved had she wished to, for gods are very terrifying creatures and not to be antagonized. If Che, Lord Forest, wished to carry her away, it would be certain death to oppose him; that she knew, and so Itzl Cha lay very quietly on the broad shoulder of her rescuer.

Tarzan could tell by the diminishing volume of the sounds of pursuit that he had thrown the mob off his trail. He soon reached the city wall at some distance from any gate. Alone he could have gained the top; but burdened with the girl, he could not; so he looked about him quickly for some means of scaling it.

Just inside the wall was a narrow street, about fifteen feet wide, which was lined with buildings and sheds of different heights, and here Tarzan saw his way. To reach the roof of a low shed with the girl was no feat for the ape man, and from this shed he went to the roof of a higher structure, and then to another which was on a level with the top of the city wall.

Itzl Cha, who had kept her eyes tightly closed most of the time now opened them again. She saw that Che, Lord Forest, had carried her to the roof of a building. Now he was running swiftly across the roof toward the narrow street which lay just within the wall. He did not slacken his speed as he approached the edge of the roof; and that made Itzl Cha close her eyes again very tightly, for she knew that they both were going to be dashed to death on the pavement in the street below.

At the edge of the roof, Tarzan leaped up and outward, alighting on the top of the wall on the opposite side of the street. Below him was the thatched roof of a laborer's hut, and to this he leaped, and from there to the ground. A moment later, with Itzl Cha gasping for breath, he was trotting across the cultivated fields toward the forest.

## XV

Life in the camp of the castaways was well ordered and run along military lines, for Colonel Leigh had taken full command. Lacking bugles, he had set up the ship's bell, which rang at six o'clock each morning, a clanging imitation of reveille; it summoned the company to mess three times a day, and announced tattoo at nine, and taps at ten each night. Sentries guarded the camp twenty-four hours each day, and working parties policed it, or chopped wood, or gathered such natural foods as the jungle afforded. It was indeed a model camp, from which fishing parties rowed out upon the lagoon daily, and hunting parties went into the forest in search of game, wherewith to vary the monotony of their fruit and vegetable diet. It was the duty of the women to keep their own quarters in order and do such mending as might be required.

Tarzan's mysterious disappearance and protracted absence was the subject of considerable conversation. "It is good riddance," said Penelope Leigh. "Never, since I first saw that terrible creature, have I felt safe until now."

"I don't see how you can say such a thing," said her niece; "I should feel very much safer were he here."

"One never knew when he might take it into his head to eat one," insisted Mrs. Leigh.

"I was shut up with him for days in that cage," said Janette Laon; "and he never showed me even the slightest incivility, let alone threatening to harm me."

"Hmph!" snorted Penelope, who had never as yet condescended to recognize the existence of Janette, let alone speak to her. She had made up her mind on first sight that Janette was a loose woman; and when Penelope Leigh made up her mind, not even an act of Parliament might change it ordinarily.

"Before he went away, he had been making weapons," recalled Patricia, "and I suppose he went into the forest to hunt; perhaps a lion or a tiger got him."

"Serve him right," snapped Mrs. Leigh. "The very idea of turning all those wild beasts loose on this island with us. It will be a miracle if we are not all devoured."

"He went out into the jungle without any firearms," mused Janette Laon, half to herself; "I heard Colonel Leigh say that not even a pistol was missing. Just think of going into that jungle where he knew all those ferocious beasts were, and with only a gaff and some homemade arrows and a bow."

Mrs. Leigh hated to acknowledge any interest in Janette Laon's conversation, but she couldn't resist the temptation of saying, "He's probably a half-wit; most of these wild men are."

"I wouldn't know," said Janette Laon sweetly, "never having had an occasion to associate with any."

Mrs. Leigh sniffed, and Patricia turned her back to hide a smile.

Algernon Wright-Smith, Captain Bolton, and Dr. Crouch were hunting. They had gone northward into the jungle hoping to bring fresh meat back to the camp. They were following a dim trail in the damp earth of which the footprints of pig could occasionally be identified, and these gave them hope and lured them on.

"Nasty place to meet a tusker," remarked Crouch.

"Rather," agreed Algy.

"Look here!" exclaimed Bolton, who was in advance.

"What is it?" asked Crouch.

"The pug of a tiger or a lion," replied Bolton; "fresh too—the blighter must just have crossed the trail."

Crouch and Algy examined the imprint of the beast's pug in the soft earth. "Tiger," said Crouch; "no doubt about it—I've seen too many of them to be mistaken."

"Rotten place to meet old stripes," said Algy; "I—," a coughing grunt interrupted him. "I say!" he exclaimed, "there's the beggar now."

"Where?" demanded Bolton.

"Off there to the left," said Crouch.

"Can't see a bloody thing," said Algy.

"I think we should go back," said Bolton; "we wouldn't have a chance if that fellow charged; one of us would be sure to be killed—maybe more."

"I think you're right," said Crouch; "I don't like the idea of having that fellow between us and camp." There was a sudden crashing in the underbrush a short distance from them.

"My God!" exclaimed Algy, "here he comes!" as he threw down his gun and clambered into a tree.

The other men followed Algy's example and none too soon, for they were scarcely out of harm's way when a great Bengal tiger broke from cover and leaped into the trail. He stood looking around for a moment, and then he caught sight of the treed men and growled. His terrible yellow-green eyes and his snarling face were turned up toward them.

Crouch commenced to laugh, and the other two men looked at him in surprise. "I'm glad there was no one here to see that," he said; "it would have been a terrible blow to British prestige."

"What the devil else could we do?" demanded Bolton. "You know as well as I do that we didn't have a ghost of a show against him, even with three guns."

"Of course not," said Algy; "couldn't have got a sight of him to fire at until he was upon us. Certainly was lucky for us there were some trees we could climb in a hurry; good old trees; I always did like trees."

The tiger came forward growling, and when he was beneath the tree in which Algy was perched, he crouched and sprang.

"By jove!" exclaimed Algy, climbing higher; "the beggar almost got me."

Twice more the tiger sprang for one of them, and then he walked back along the trail a short distance and lay down patiently.

"The beggar's got us to rights," said Bolton.

"He won't stay there forever," said Crouch.

Bolton shook his head. "I hope not," he said, "but they have an amazing amount of patience; I know a chap who was treed by one all night in Bengal."

"Oh, I say, he couldn't do that, you know," objected Algy. "What does he take us for—a lot of bally asses? Does he think we're coming down there to be eaten up?"

"He probably thinks that when we are ripe, we'll fall off, like apples and things."

"This is deucedly uncomfortable," said Algy after a while; "I'm pretty well fed up with it. I wish I had my gun."

"It's right down there at the foot of your tree," said Crouch; "why don't you go down and get it?"

"I say, old thing!" exclaimed Algy; "I just had a brain-storm. Watch." He took off his shirt, commenced tearing it into strips which he tied together, and when he had a long string of this he made a slip noose at one end; then he came down to a lower branch and dropped the noose down close to the muzzle of his gun, which, because of the way in which the weapon had fallen, was raised a couple of inches from the ground.

"Clever?" demanded Algy.

"Very," said Bolton. The tiger is admiring your ingenuity; see him watching you?"

"If that noose catches behind the sight, I can draw the bally thing up here, and then I'll let old stripes have what for."

"You should have been an engineer, Algy," said Crouch.

"My mother wanted me to study for the Church," said Algy, "and my father wanted me to go into the diplomatic corps—both make me bored; so I just played tennis instead."

"And you're rotten at that," said Crouch, laughing.

"Righto, old thing!" agreed Algy. "Look! I have it."

After much fishing, the noose had slipped over the muzzle of the gun, and as Algy pulled gently, it tightened below the sight; then he started drawing the weapon up towards him.

He had it within a foot of his hand when the tiger leaped to his feet with a roar and charged. As the beast sprang into the air towards Algy, the man dropped everything and scrambled towards safety, as the raking talons swept within an inch of his foot.

"Whe-e-ew!" exclaimed Algy, as he reached a higher branch.

"Now you've even lost your shirt," said Crouch.

The tiger stood looking up for a moment, growling and lashing his tail, and then he went back and lay down again.

"I believe the beggar is going to keep us here all night," said Algy.

## XVI

Krause and his fellows had not gone two days march from the camp of the castaways, as Tarzan had ordered them to do. They had gone only about four miles up the coast, where they had camped by another stream where it emptied into the ocean. They were a bitter and angry company as they squatted disconsolately upon the beach and ate the fruit that they had made the Lascars gather. They sweated and fumed for a couple of days and made plans and quarrelled. Both Krause and Schmidt wished to command, and Schmidt won out because Krause was the bigger coward and was afraid of the madman. Abdullah Abu Néjm sat apart and hated them all. Oubanovitch talked a great deal in a loud tone of voice and argued that they should all be comrades and that nobody should command. By a single thread of common interest were they held together—their hatred of Tarzan, because he had sent them away without arms or ammunition.

"We could go back at night and steal what we need," suggested Oubanovitch.

"I have been thinking that same thing, myself," said Schmidt. "You go back now, Oubanovitch, and reconnoiter. You can hide in the jungle just outside their camp and get a good lay of the land, so that we shall know just where the rifles are kept."

"You go yourself," said Oubanovitch, "you can't order me around."

"I'm in command," screamed Schmidt, springing to his feet.

Oubanovitch stood up too. He was a big hulking brute, much larger than Schmidt. "So what!" he demanded.

"There's no sense in fighting among ourselves," said Krause. "Why don't you send a Lascar?"

"If I had a gun this dirty Communist would obey me," Schmidt grumbled, and then he called to one of the Lascar sailors. "Come here, Chuldrup," he ordered.

The Lascar slouched forward, sullen and scowling. He hated Schmidt; but all his life he had taken orders from white men, and the habit was strong upon him.

"You go other camp," Schmidt directed; "hide in jungle; see where guns, bullets kept."

"No go," said Chuldrup; "tiger in jungle."

"The hell you won't go!" exclaimed Schmidt, and knocked the sailor down. "I'll teach you." The sailor came to his feet, a boiling caldron of hate. He wanted to kill the white man, but he was still afraid. "Now get out of here, you heathen dog," Schmidt yelled at him; "and see that you don't come back until you find out what you want to know." Chuldrup turned and walked away, and a moment later the jungle closed behind him.

"I say!" exclaimed Algy. "What's the blighter doing now?" The tiger had arisen and was standing, ears forward, looking back along the trail. He cocked his head on one side, listening.

"He hears something coming," said Bolton.

"There he goes," said Crouch, as the tiger slunk into the underbrush beside the trail.

"Now's our chance," said Algy.

"He didn't go far," said Bolton; "he's right there; I can see him."

"Trying to fool us," said Crouch.

Chuldrup was very much afraid; he was afraid of the jungle, but he was more afraid to return to Schmidt without the information the man wanted. He stopped for a moment to think the matter over; should he go back and hide in the jungle for a while close to Schmidt's camp and then when there had been time for him to fulfill his mission go to Schmidt and make up a story about the location of the guns and bullets?

Chuldrup scratched his head, and then the light of a great idea broke upon him; he would go to the camp of the Englishmen, tell them what Schmidt was planning, and ask them to let him remain with them. That, he knew, was one of the best ideas that he had ever had in his life; and so he turned and trotted happily along the trail.

"Something is coming," whispered Crouch; "I can hear it," and a moment later Chuldrup came trotting into view.

All three men shouted warnings simultaneously, but too late. As the Lascar stopped amazed and looked up at them, momentarily uncomprehending, a great tiger leaped from the underbrush and rearing up above the terrified man seized him by the shoulder.

Chuldrup screamed; the great beast shook him and then turned and dragged him off into the underbrush, while the three Englishmen, horrified, looked on helplessly.

For a few moments they could hear the screams of the man mingling with the growls of the tiger and then the screams ceased.

"My God!" exclaimed Algy, "that was awful."

"Yes," said Bolton, "but it's our chance; he won't bother anything now that doesn't go near his kill."

Gingerly and quietly they descended to the ground, picked up their rifles, and started back toward camp; but all three were shaken by the tragedy they had witnessed.

In the camp the day's work was done; even Colonel Leigh could find nothing more to keep the men busy.

"I must be getting old," he said to his wife.

"Getting?" she asked. "Are you just discovering it?"

The Colonel smiled indulgently; he was always glad when Penelope was herself. Whenever she said anything pleasant or kindly he was worried. "Yes," he continued, "I must be slipping; I can't think of a damn thing for these men to do."

"It seems to me there should be plenty to do around here," said Penelope; "I am always busy."

"I think the men deserve a little leisure," said Patricia; "they've been working steadily ever since we've gotten here."

"There's nothing that breeds discontent more surely than idleness," said the Colonel; "but I'm going to let them knock off for the rest of the day."

Hans de Groote and Janette Laon were sitting together on the beach talking.

"Life is funny," said the man. "Just a few weeks ago, I

was looking forward to seeing New York City for the first time—young, fancy-free, and with three months pay in my pocket; what a time I was planning there! And now here I am somewhere in the Pacific Ocean on an island that no one ever heard of—and that's not the worst of it."

"And what is the worst of it?" asked Janette.

"That I like it," replied de Groote.

"Like it!" she exclaimed. "But why do you like it?"

"Because you are here," he said.

The girl looked at him in surprise. "I don't understand," she said; "you certainly can't mean that the way it sounds."

"But I do, Janette," he said; "I—," his tanned face flushed. "Why is it that those three words are so hard to say when you mean them?"

She reached out and placed her hand on his. "You mustn't say them," she said; "you mustn't ever say them—to me."

"Why?" he demanded.

"You know what I have been—kicking around Singapore, Saigon, Batavia."

"I love you," said Hans de Groote, and then Janette Laon burst into tears; it had been long since she had cried except in anger or disappointment.

"I won't let you," she said; "I won't let you."

"Don't you—love me a little, Janette?" he asked.

"I won't tell you," she said; "I won't ever tell you."

De Groote pressed her hand and smiled. "You have told me," he said.

And then they were interrupted by Patricia's voice crying, "Why, Algy, where is your shirt?"

The hunters had returned, and the Europeans gathered around to hear their story. When they had finished the Colonel harrumphed. "That settles it," he said; "there will be no more hunting in the jungle; no one would have a chance against a tiger or a lion in that tangle of undergrowth."

"It's all your fault, William," snapped Mrs. Leigh; "you should have taken complete command; you should not have permitted that wildman to turn those beasts loose on us."

"I still think that it was quite the sporting thing to do," said the Colonel, "and don't forget that it was quite as dangerous for him as for us. As far as we know the poor devil may have been killed by one of them already."

"And serve him quite right," said Mrs. Leigh; "anyone who will run around the way he does in the presence of ladies has no business to live—at least not among decent people."

"I think the fellow was just a little bit of all right," said the Colonel, "and don't forget, Penelope, if it had not been for him, we would probably be a great deal worse off than we are now."

"Don't forget, Aunt Penelope, that he rescued you from the Saigon."

"I am doing my best to forget it," said Mrs. Leigh.

# XVII

When Itzl Cha realized that she was being carried off toward the forest, she was not quite sure what her feelings were. Back in Chichen Itza was certain death, for the gods could not be lightly robbed of their victims; and, were she ever to return, she knew that she would be again offered up in sacrifice. What lay ahead she could not even guess; but Itzl Cha was young and life was sweet; and perhaps Che, Lord Forest, would not kill her.

When'they reached the forest Che did an amazing thing: he leaped to the low branch of a tree and then swung upward, carrying her swiftly high above the ground. Now indeed was Itzl Cha terrified.

Presently Che stopped and voiced a long drawn-out call— an eerie cry that echoed through the forest; then he went on.

The girl had summoned sufficient courage to keep her eyes open, but presently she saw something that made her wish to close them again; however, fascinated, she continued to look at two grotesque creatures swinging through the trees to meet them, jabbering as they came.

Che replied in the same strange jargon, and Itzl Cha knew that she was listening to the language of the gods, for these two must indeed be the two earth gods of whom Thak Chan had spoken. When these two reached Che, all three stopped and spoke to each other in that language she could not understand. It was then that Itzl Cha chanced to glance down at the ground into a little clearing upon the edge of which they were, and there she saw the body of a terrible beast; and she knew that it was the same one from which Che had rescued Thak Chan, the hunter.

She wished that the skeptics in Chichen Itza could see all that she had seen, for then they would know that these were indeed gods; and they would be sorry and frightened because they had treated Lord Forest as they had.

Her divine rescuer carried her to a mountain trail, and

there he set her down upon the ground and let her walk. Now she had a good look at him; how beautiful he was! Indeed a god. The two earth gods waddled along with them, and from being afraid Itzl Cha commenced to be very proud when she thought of the company in which she was. What other girl in Chichen Itza had ever walked abroad with three gods?

Presently they came to a place where the trail seemed to end, disappearing over the brink of a terrifying precipice; but Che, Lord Forest, did not hesitate; he merely took Itzl Cha across that broad shoulder again and clambered down the declivity with as great ease as did the two earth gods.

However, Itzl Cha could not help but be terrified when she looked down; and so she closed her eyes tightly and held her breath and pressed her little body very close to that of Che, Lord Forest, who had become to her something akin to a haven of refuge.

But at last they reached the bottom and once again Lord Forest raised his voice. What he said sounded to Itzl Cha like "Yud, Tantor, yud!" And that was exactly what it was: "Come, Tantor, Come!"

Very shortly, Itzl Cha heard a sound such as she had never heard before—a sound that no other Mayan had ever heard; the trumpeting of an elephant.

By this time, Itzl Cha thought that she had seen all the miracles that there were to be seen in the world, but when a great bull elephant broke through the forest, toppling the trees that were in his path, little Itzl Cha screamed and fainted.

When Itzl Cha regained consciousness, she did not immediately open her eyes. She was conscious of an arm about her, and that her back was resting against a human body; but what caused that strange motion, and what was that rough surface that she straddled with her bare legs?

Fearfully, Itzl Cha opened her eyes; but she immediately screamed and closed them again. She was sitting on the head of that terrible beast she had seen!

Lord Forest was sitting behind her, and it was his arm that was around her, preventing her from falling to the ground. The earth gods were swinging along in the trees beside them; they seemed to be scolding. It was all too much for little Itzl Cha; in a brief hour or two, she had experienced a lifetime of thrills and adventure.

The afternoon was drawing to a close. Lum Kip was preparing dinner for the Europeans. This was not a difficult procedure; there was fish to fry, and some tubers to boil. Fruit made up the balance of the menu. Lum Kip was cheerful and happy; he liked to work for the foreign devils; they treated him well, and the work was not nearly as arduous as chopping wood.

The two girls in the party and most of the men were sitting on the ground, talking over the events of the day, especially the hunting trip which had ended in tragedy. Patricia wondered if they would ever see Tarzan again, and that started them talking about the wildman and his probable fate. The Colonel was in his hut shaving, and his wife was sitting out in front of it with her mending, when something attracted her attention, and, looking toward the forest she voiced a single ear-piercing shriek and fainted. Instantly everyone was on his feet; the Colonel, his face half lathered, rushed from the hut.

Patricia Leigh-Burden cried, "Oh, my God, look!"

Coming out of the forest was a great bull elephant, and on its neck sat Tarzan holding an almost naked girl in front of him; two orang-utans waddled along at a safe distance on one side. No wonder Penelope Leigh had fainted. The elephant stopped a few paces outside the forest; the sight of all these people was too much for him, and he would come no farther. Tarzan, with the girl in his arms, slipped to the ground, and, holding her by the hand, led her toward the camp.

Itzl Cha felt that these must all be gods, but much of her fear was gone now, for Lord Forest had offered her no harm, nor had the earth gods, nor had that strange enormous beast on which she had ridden through the forest.

Patricia Leigh-Burden looked questioningly and a little suspiciously at the girl walking at Tarzan's side. One of the sailors working nearby said to another, "That fellow is a fast worker." Patricia heard it, and her lips tightened.

Tarzan was greeted by silence, but it was the silence of surprise. The Colonel was working over his wife, and presently she opened her eyes. "Where is he?" she whispered. "That creature! You must get him out of camp immediately, William, he and that wanton girl with him. Both of them together didn't have on enough clothes to cover a baby decently. I suppose he went off somewhere and stole a woman, an Indian woman at that."

"Oh, quiet, Penelope," said the Colonel, a little irritably; "you don't know anything about it and neither do I."

"Well, you'd better make it your businesss to find out," snapped Mrs. Leigh. "I don't intend to permit Patricia to remain in the same camp with such people, nor shall I remain."

Tarzan walked directly to Patricia Leigh-Burden. "I want you to look after this girl," he said.

"I?" demanded Patricia haughtily.

"Yes, you," he replied.

"Come, come," said the Colonel, still half lathered, "what is the meaning of all this, sir?"

"There's a city to the south of us," said Tarzan, "a good-sized city, and they have some heathen rites in which they sacrifice human beings; this girl was about to be sacrificed, when I was lucky enough to be able to take her away. She can't go back there because of course they would kill her; so we'll have to look after her. If your niece won't do it, I'm sure that Janette will."

"Of course I'll look after her," said Patricia; "who said that I wouldn't?"

"Put some clothes on the thing," said Mrs. Leigh; "this is absolutely disgraceful."

Tarzan looked at her with disgust. "It is your evil mind that needs clothes," he said.

Penelope Leigh's jaws dropped. She stood there open-mouthed and speechless for a moment; then she wheeled about and stamped into her hut.

"I say, old thing," said Algy, "how the deuce did you get that elephant to let you ride on his head; that was one of the wild African bulls?"

"How do you get your friends to do you favors?" asked Tarzan.

"But, I say, you know, old thing, I haven't any friends like that."

"That is too bad," said the ape man. Then he turned to the Colonel, "We must take every precaution against attack;" he said; "there were many warriors in that city, and I have no doubts but that a search will be made for this girl; eventually they will find our camp. Of course they are not accustomed to firearms, and if we are always on the alert, we have little to fear; but I suggest that only very strong parties be allowed to go into the jungle."

"I have just issued orders that no one is to go into the jungle," replied the Colonel. "Captain Bolton, Dr. Crouch, and Mr. Wright-Smith were attacked by one of your tigers today."

## XVIII

For six weeks the life in the camp dragged on monotonously and without incident; and during that time, Patricia Leigh-Burden taught Itzl Cha to speak and understand enough English so that the little Mayan girl could carry on at least a sketchy conversation with the others, while Tarzan devoted much of his time to learning the Maya tongue from her. Tarzan, alone of the company, ventured occasionally into the jungle; and, from these excursions, he often returned with a wild pig.

His absence from camp always aroused Penelope Leigh's ire. "He is impudent and insubordinate," she complained to her husband. "You gave strict orders that no one was to go into the jungle, and he deliberately disobeys you. You should make an example of him."

"What do you suggest that I do with him, my dear?" asked the Colonel. "Should he be drawn and quartered, or merely shot at sunrise?"

"Don't try to be facetious, William; it does not become you. You should simply insist that he obey the regulations that you have laid down."

"And go without fresh pork?" asked the Colonel.

"I do not like pork," snapped Mrs. Leigh. "Furthermore, I do not like the goings-on around this camp; Mr. de Groote is far too intimate with that French woman, and the wildman is always around that Indian girl. Look at them now—always talking together; I can imagine what he is saying to her."

"He is trying to learn her language," explained the Colonel; "something that may prove very valuable to us later on, if we ever have any dealings with her people."

"Hmph!" snorted Mrs. Leigh; "a fine excuse. And the way they dress! If I can find some goods in the ship's stores, I shall make her a Mother Hubbard; and as for him—you should do something about that. And now look; there goes Patricia over to talk to them. William, you must put a stop to all this nonsense—it is indecent."

Colonel William Cecil Hugh Percival Leigh sighed; his was not an entirely happy existence. Many of the men were becoming restless, and there were some who had commenced to question his right to command them. He rather questioned it himself, but he knew that conditions would become unbearable if there were no one in authority. Of course Algy, Bolton, Tibbet, and Crouch backed him up, as did de Groote and Tarzan. It was upon Tarzan that he depended most, for he realized that here was a man who would brook no foolishness in the event of mutiny. And now his wife wanted him to insist that this half-savage man wear trousers. The Colonel sighed again.

Patricia sat down beside Tarzan and Itzl Cha. "How goes the class in Mayan?" she asked.

"Itzl Cha says that I am doing splendidly," replied Tarzan.

"And Itzl Cha is mastering English, after a fashion," said Patricia; "she and I can almost carry on an intelligent conversation. She has told me some very interesting things. Do you know why they were going to sacrifice her?"

"To some god, I suppose," replied Tarzan.

"Yes, to a god called Che, Lord Forest, to appease him for the affront done him by a man that claimed you were Che, Lord Forest.

"Itzl Cha is, of course, positive that she was rescued by no one less than Che, Lord Forest; and she says that many of her people will believe that too. She says that it is the first time in the history of her people that a god has come and taken alive the sacrifice being offered to him. It has made a deep impression on her and no one can ever convince her that you are not Che.

"Her own father offered her as a sacrifice in order to win favor with the gods," continued Patricia. "It is simply horrible, but it is their way; Itzl Cha says that parents often do this; although slaves and prisoners of war are usually the victims."

"She has told me a number of interesting things about her people and about the island," said Tarzan. "The island is called Uxmal, after a city in Yucatan from which her people migrated hundreds of years ago."

"They must be Mayas then," said Patricia.

"That is very interesting," said Dr. Crouch, who had joined

them. "From what you have told us of your experiences in their city, and from what Itzl Cha has told us, it is evident that they have preserved their religion and their culture almost intact throughout the centuries since the migration. What a field this would be for the anthropologist and the archaeologist. If you could establish friendly relations with them, we might be able to solve the riddles of the hieroglyphs an their stelae and temples in Central America and South America."

"As the chances are that we shall be here all the rest of our lives," Patricia reminded him, "our knowledge would do the world very little good."

"I cannot believe that we shall never be rescued," said Dr. Crouch. "By the way, Tarzan, is this village that you visited the only one on the island?"

"I don't know as to that," replied the ape man, "but these Mayans are not the only people here. At the northern end of the island, there is a settlement of what Itzl Cha calls 'very bad people.' The history of the island, handed down largely by word of mouth, indicates that survivors of a shipwreck intermarried with the aborigines of the island, and it is their descendents who live in this settlement; but they do not fraternize with the aborigines who live in the central part of the island."

"You mean that there is a native population here?" asked Dr. Crouch.

"Yes, and we are camped right on the south-western edge of their domain. I have never gone far enough into their country to see any of them, but Itzl Cha says that they are very savage cannibals."

"What a lovely place fate selected for us to be marooned," remarked Patricia, "and then to make it all the cozier, you had to turn a lot of lions and tigers loose in it." Tarzan smiled.

"At least we shall not perish from ennui," remarked Janette Laon.

Colonel Leigh, Algy, and Bolton sauntered up, and then de Groote joined the party. "Some of the men just came to me," said the Dutchman, "and wanted me to ask you, Colonel, if they could try to break up the Saigon and build a boat to get away from here. They said they would rather take a chance of dying at sea than spending the rest of their lives here."

"I don't know that I can blame them," said the Colonel. "What do you think of it, Bolton?"

"It might be done," replied the Captain.

"Anyway, it will keep them busy," said the Colonel; "and if they were doing something they wanted to do, they wouldn't be complaining all the time."

"I don't know where they would build it," said Bolton. "They certainly can't build it on the reef; and it wouldn't do any good to build it on shore, for the water in the lagoon would be too shallow to float it."

"There is deep water in a cove about a mile north of here," said Tarzan, "and no reef."

"By the time the blighters have taken the Saigon apart," said Algy, "and carried it a mile along the coast, they'll be too exhausted to build a boat."

"Or too old," suggested Patricia.

"Who's going to design the boat?" asked the Colonel.

"The men have asked me to," replied de Groote; "my father is a shipbuilder, and I worked in his yard before I went to sea."

"It's not a bad idea," said Crouch; "do you think you can build a boat large enough to take us all?"

"It depends upon how much of the Saigon we can salvage," replied de Groote. "If we should have another bad storm soon, the whole ship might break up."

Algernon Wright-Smith made a sweeping gesture toward the forest. "We have plenty of lumber there," he said, "if the Saigon fails us."

"That would be some job," said Bolton.

"Well, we've got all our lives to do it in, old thing," Algy reminded him.

## XIX

When two days had passed and Chuldrup had not returned, Schmidt drove another Lascar into the forest with orders to go to Tarzan's camp and get information about the guns and ammunition.

The Lascars had made a separate camp, a short distance from that occupied by Schmidt, Krause, Oubanovitch, and the Arab. They had been very busy, but none of the four men in the smaller camp had paid any attention to them, merely summoning one of them when they wanted to give any orders.

The second man whom Schmidt had sent in the forest never returned. Schmidt was furious, and on the third day he ordered two men to go. They stood sullenly before him, listening. When he had finished they turned and walked back to their own camp. Schmidt watched them; he saw them sit down with their fellows. He waited a moment to see if they would start, but they did not. Then he started toward their camp, white with rage.

"I'll teach them," he muttered; "I'll show them who's boss here—the brown devils;" but when he approached them, fifteen Lascars stood up to face him, and he saw that they were armed with bows and arrows and wooden spears. This was the work that had kept them so busy for several days.

Schmidt and the Lascars stood facing one another for several moments; then one of the latter said, "What do you want here?"

There were fifteen of them, fifteen sullen, scowling men, all well armed.

"Aren't you two men going to find out about the guns and ammunition so that we can get them?" he asked.

"No," said one of the two. "You want to know, you go. We no take orders any more. Get out. Go back to your own camp."

"This is mutiny," blustered Schmidt.

"Get out," said a big Lascar, and fitted an arrow to his bow.

Schmidt turned and slunk away.

"What's the matter?" asked Krause, when Schmidt reached his own camp.

"The devils have mutinied," replied Schmidt, "and they are all armed—made bows and arrows and spears for themselves."

"The uprising of the proletariat!" exclaimed Oubanovitch. "I shall join them and lead them. It is glorious, glorious; the world revolution has reached even here!"

"Shut up!" said Schmidt; "you give me a pain."

"Wait until I organize my glorious revolutionaries," cried Oubanovitch; "then you will sing a different song; then it will be 'Comrade Oubanovitch, this, and 'Comrade Oubanovitch, that.' Now I go to my comrades who have risen in their might and cast the yoke of Capitalism from their necks."

He crossed jubilantly to the camp of the Lascars. "Comrades!" he cried. "Congratulations on your glorious achievement. I have come to lead you on to greater victories. We will march on the camp of the Capitalists who threw us out. We will liquidate them, and we will take all their guns and ammunition and all their supplies."

Fifteen scowling men looked at him in silence for a moment; then one of them said, "Get out."

"But!" exclaimed Oubanovitch, "I have come to join you; together we will go on to glorious—"

"Get out," repeated the Lascar.

Oubanovitch hesitated until several of them started toward him; then he turned and went back to the other camp. "Well, Comrade," said Schmidt, with a sneer, "is the revolution over?"

"They are stupid fools," said Oubanovitch.

That night the four men had to attend to their own fire, which the Lascars had kept burning for them in the past as a safeguard against wild beasts; and they had had to gather the wood for it, too. Now it devolved upon them to take turns standing guard.

"Well, Comrade," said Schmidt to Oubanovitch, "how do

you like revolutions now that you are on the other side of one?"

The Lascars, having no white man to command them, all went to sleep and let their fire die out. Abdullah Abu Néjm was on guard in the smaller camp when he heard a series of ferocious growls from the direction of the Lascar's camp, and then a scream of pain and terror. The other three men awoke and sprang to their feet.

"What is it?" demanded Schmidt

"El adrea, Lord of the Broad Head," replied the Arab.

"What's that?" asked Oubanovitch.

"A lion," said Krause; "he got one of them."

The screams of the unfortunate victim was still blasting the silence of the night, but they were farther from the camp of the Lascars now, as the lion dragged his prey farther away from the presence of the other men. Presently the screams ceased, and then came an even more grisly and horrifying sound—the tearing and rending of flesh and bones mingled with the growls of the carnivore.

Krause piled more wood upon the fire. "That damn wild-man," he said—"turning those beasts loose here."

"Serves you right," said Schmidt; "you had no business catching a white man and putting him in a cage."

"It was Abdullah's idea," whined Krause; "I never would have thought of it if he hadn't put it into my head."

There was no more sleep in the camp that night. They could hear the lion feeding until daylight, and then in the lesser darkness of dawn, they saw him rise from his kill and go to the river to drink; then he disappeared into the jungle.

"He will lie up for the day," said Abdullah, "but he will come out again and feed."

As Abdullah ceased speaking, a foul sound came from the edge of the jungle, and two forms slunk out; the hyenas had scented the lion's kill, and presently they were tearing at what was left of the Lascar.

The next night, the Lascars built no fire at all; and another was taken. "The fools!" exclaimed Krause; "that lion has got the habit by now, and none of us will ever be safe again here."

"They are fatalists," said Schmidt; "they believe that whatever is foreordained to happen must happen, and that nothing they can do about it can prevent it."

"Well, I'm no fatalist," said Krause. "I'm going to sleep in a tree after this," and he spent the next day building a platform in a tree at the edge of the forest, setting an example which the other three men were quick to follow. Even the Lascars were impressed, and that night the lion came and roared through empty camps.

"I've stood all of this that I can," said Krause; "I'm going back and see that fellow, Tarzan. I'll promise anything if he'll let us stay in his camp."

"How are you going to get there?" asked Schmidt. "I wouldn't walk through that jungle again for twenty million marks."

"I don't intend to walk through the jungle," said Krause. "I'm going to follow the beach. I could always run out into the ocean if I met anything."

"I think El adrea would be kinder to us than Tarzan of the Apes," said the Arab.

"I never did anything to him," said Oubanovitch; "he ought to let me come back."

"He's probably afraid you'd start a revolution," said Schmidt. But they finally decided to try it; and early the next morning, they set out along the beach toward the other camp.

# XX

Chand, the Lascar, watched Krause and his three companions start along the beach in the direction of Camp Saigon. "They are going to the other camp," he said to his fellows. "Come, we will go too;" and a moment later they were trailing along the beach in the wake of the others.

In Camp Saigon, Tarzan was eating his breakfast alone. He had arisen early, for he had planned a full day's work. Only Lum Kip was astir, going about his work quietly preparing breakfast. Presently Patricia Leigh-Burden came from her hut and joined Tarzan, sitting down beside him.

"You are up early this morning," she said.

"I am always earlier than the others," he replied, "but today I had a special reason; I want to get an early start."

"Where are you going?" she asked.

"I'm going exploring," he replied, "I want to see what is on the other side of the island."

Patricia leaned forward eagerly, placing a hand upon his knee. "Oh, may I go with you?" she asked. "I'd love it."

From the little shelter that had been built especially for her, Itzl Cha watched them. Her black eyes narrowed and snapped, and she clenched her little hands tightly.

"You couldn't make it, Patricia," said Tarzan, "not the way I travel."

"I've hiked through jungles in India," she said.

"No," he said, quite definitely; "traveling on the ground in there is too dangerous. I suppose you've heard it mentioned that there are wild animals there."

"Then if it's dangerous you shouldn't go," she said, "carrying nothing but a silly bow and some arrows. Let me go along with a rifle; I'm a good shot, and I've hunted tigers in India."

Tarzan rose, and Patricia jumped to her feet, placing her hands on his shoulders. "Please don't go," she begged, "I'm afraid for you," but he only laughed and turned and trotted off toward the jungle.

Patricia watched him until he swung into a tree and disappeared; then she swished around angrily and went to her hut. "I'll show him," she muttered under her breath.

Presently she emerged with a rifle and ammunition. Itzl Cha watched her as she entered the jungle at the same place that Tarzan had, right at the edge of the little stream. The little Mayan girl bit her lips, and the tears came to her eyes—tears of frustration and anger. Lum Kip, working around the cook fire, commenced to hum to himself.

Chal Yip Xiu, the high priest, was still furious about the theft of Itzl Cha from beneath the sacred sacrificial knife. "The temple has been defiled," he growled, "and the gods will be furious."

"Perhaps not," said Cit Coh Xiu, the king; "perhaps after all that was indeed Che, Lord Forest."

Chal Yip Xiu looked at the king, disgustedly. "He was only one of the strangers that Xatl Din saw on the beach. If you would not arouse the anger of the gods, you should send a force of warriors to the camp of the strangers, to bring Itzl Cha back, for that is where she will be found."

"Perhaps you are right," said the king; "at least it will do no harm," and he sent for Xatl Din and ordered him to take a hundred warriors and go to the camp of the strangers and get Itzl Cha. "With a hundred warriors, you should be able to kill many of them and bring back prisoners to Chichen Itza."

Tibbett, with a boatload of sailors, was rowing out to the reef to continue the work of salvaging lumber from the Saigon, as the other members of the party came out for their breakfast. Itzl Cha sat silent and sullen, eating very little, for she had lost her appetite. Janette Laon came and sat beside de Groote, and Penelope Leigh looked at them down her nose.

"Is Patricia up yet, Janette?" asked the Colonel.

Janette looked around the company. "Why, yes," she said, "isn't she here? She was gone when I woke up."

"Where in the world can that girl be?" demanded Penelope Leigh.

"Oh, she must be nearby," said the Colonel, but, as he called her name aloud, it was evident that he was perturbed.

"And that creature is gone too!" exclaimed Mrs. Leigh. "I knew that something terrible like this was going to happen sooner or later, William, if you permitted that man to remain in camp."

"Now, just what has happened, Penelope?" asked the Colonel.

"Why he's abducted her, that's what's happened."

Lum Kip, who was putting a platter of rice on the table, overheard the conversation and volunteered, "Tarzan, she, go that way," pointing toward the northeast; "Plateecie, him go that way," and pointed in the same direction.

"Maybe Pat abducted him," suggested Algy.

"Don't be ridiculous, Algernon," snapped Mrs. Leigh. "It is quite obvious what happened—the creature enticed her into the jungle."

"They talked long," said Itzl Cha, sullenly. "They go different times; they meet in jungle."

"How can you sit there, William, and permit that Indian girl to intimate that your niece arranged an assignation in the jungle with that impossible creature."

"Well," said the Colonel, "if Pat's in the jungle, I pray to high heaven that Tarzan is with her."

Pat followed a stream that ran for a short distance in a northeasterly direction, and when it turned southeast, she continued to follow it, not knowing that Tarzan had taken to the trees and was swinging rapidly through them almost due east toward the other side of the island. The ground rose rapidly now, and the little stream tumbled excitedly down toward the ocean. Pat realized that she was being a stubborn fool, but, being stubborn, she decided to climb the mountain a short distance to get a view of the island. It was a hard climb, and the trees constantly shut out any view, but the girl kept on until she came to a level ledge which ran around a shoulder of the mountain. As she was pretty well winded by this time, she sat down to rest.

"I should think some of you men would go out and look for Patricia," said Mrs. Leigh.

"I'll go," said Algy, "but I don't know where to look for the old girl."

"Who's that coming along the beach?" said Dr. Crouch.

"Why it's Krause and Schmidt," said Bolton. "Yes, and Oubanovitch and the Arab are with him." Almost automatically the men loosened their pistols in their holsters and waited in silence as the four approached.

The men about the breakfast table had all risen and were waiting expectantly. Krause came to the point immediately. "We've come to ask you to let us come back and camp near you," he said. "We have no firearms and no protection where we are. Two of our men have gone into the jungle and never returned, and two have been taken right out of camp by lions at night. You certainly must have a heart, Colonel; you certainly won't subject fellow men to such dangers needlessly. If you will take us back, we promise to obey you and not cause any trouble."

"I'm afraid it will cause a lot of trouble when Tarzan returns and finds you here," said the Colonel.

"You should let them remain, William," said Mrs. Leigh. "You are in command here, not that Tarzan creature."

"I really think it would be inhuman to send them away," said Dr. Crouch.

"They were inhuman to us," said Janette Laon bitterly.

"Young woman," exploded Penelope, "you should be taught your place; you have nothing to say about this. The Colonel will decide."

Janette Laon shook her head hopelessly and winked at de Groote. Penelope saw the wink and exploded again. "You are an insolent baggage," she said; "you and the Indian girl and that Tarzan creature should never have been permitted in the same camp with gentlefolk."

"If you will permit me, Penelope," said the Colonel stiffly, "I think that I can handle this matter without assistance or at least without recrimination."

"Well, all that I have to say," said Penelope, "is that you must let them remain."

"Suppose," suggested Crouch, "that we let them remain

anyway until Tarzan returns; then we can discuss the matter with him—they are more his enemies than ours."

"They are enemies to all of us," said Janette.

"You may remain, Krause," said the Colonel, "at least, until Tarzan returns; and see that you behave yourselves."

"We certainly shall, Colonel," replied Krause, "and thank you for letting us stay."

Patricia got a view of the ocean from the ledge where she was sitting, but she could see nothing of the island; and so, after resting, she went on a little farther. It was far more open here and very beautiful, orchids clung in gorgeous sprays to many a tree, and ginger and hibiscus grew in profusion; birds with yellow plumage and birds with scarlet winged from tree to tree. It was an idyllic, peaceful scene which soothed her nerves and obliterated the last vestige of her anger.

She was glad that she had found this quiet spot and was congratulating herself, and planning that she would come to it often, when a great tiger walked out of the underbrush and faced her. The tip of his tail was twiching nervously, and his snarling muscles had drawn his lips back from his great yellow fangs.

Patricia Leigh-Burden breathed a silent prayer as she threw her rifle to her shoulder and fired twice in rapid succession.

## XXI

"I certainly do not like the idea of having those men around here all the time," said Janette; "I am afraid of them, especially Krause."

"I'll look after him," said de Groote. "Let me know if he ever makes any advances."

"And now look!" exclaimed Janette, pointing along the beach. "Here come all those Lascars back, too. Those fellows give me the creeps."

As she ceased speaking, the report of two rifle shots came faintly but distinctly to their ears. "That must be Patricia!" exclaimed the Colonel. "She must be in trouble."

"She has probably had to shoot that creature," said Penelope hopefully.

The Colonel had run to his hut and gotten his rifle; and when he started in the direction from which the sound of the shot had come, he was followed by de Groote, Algy, Crouch, and Bolton.

As the foliage of the jungle closed about Bolton's back, Schmidt turned to Krause and grinned. "What's funny?" demanded the latter.

"Let's see what we can find in the way of rifles and ammunition," said Schmidt to the other three men. "This looks like our day."

"What are you men doing?" demanded Penelope Leigh. "Don't you dare go into those huts."

Janette started to run toward her hut to get her rifle, but Schmidt overtook her and hurled her aside. "No funny business," he warned.

The four men collected all the remaining firearms in the camp and then, at pistol points forced the Lascars to load up with such stores as Schmidt desired.

"Pretty good haul," he said to Krause. "I think we've got about everything we want now."

"Maybe you have, but I haven't," replied the animal collector; then he walked over to Janette. "Come along, sweetheart," he said; "we're going to start all over again right where we left off."

"Not I," said Janette, backing away.

Krause seized one of her arms. "Yes, you; and if you know what's good for you, you'd better not make any trouble."

The girl tried to pull away, and Krause struck her. "For heaven's sake, go along with him," cried Penelope Leigh. "Don't make a scene; I hate scenes. Anyway, you belong with him; you certainly have never belonged in my camp."

Half-stunned by the blow, Janette was dragged away; and the Colonel's wife watched them start back along the beach in the direction from which they had come.

"The Colonel shall hear about your stealing our stores, you scoundrels," she called after them.

Xatl Din and his hundred warriors came through the forest spread out in open order, that they might leave no well-marked trail; and as they came, they heard two sharp, loud sounds which seemed to come from but a short distance ahead of them. None of these men had ever heard the report of a firearm before, and so they had no idea of what it was. They crept cautiously forward, their eyes and ears constantly alert. Xatl Din was in the lead, and as he came to a more open place in the forest, he stopped suddenly, for a strange and unaccustomed sight met his eye. On the ground lay a huge, striped beast, such as he had never seen before. It was evidently dead, and above it stood a figure strangely garbed, who held a long black shiny thing that was neither bow, arrow, nor spear.

Presently Xatl Din realized that the creature was a woman; and, being an intelligent man, he surmised that the noise he had heard had come from that strange thing she held, and that with it, she had doubtless killed the huge beast which lay at her feet. Xatl Din further reasoned that if she could have killed so large and evidently ferocious an animal, she could even more easily kill men; and, therefore, he did not come out into the open, but withdrew and gave whispered instructions to his men.

Now the Mayans slipped silently around through the jungle until they had encircled Patricia, and then while Xatl Din beat on a tree with his sword to make a noise that would attract the girl's attention in his direction, two of his men slipped out of the jungle behind her, and crept noiselessly toward her.

As Patricia stood looking in the direction from which the sound had come, listening intently, arms were thrown around her from behind and her rifle was snatched from her hands; then a hundred strangely garbed warriors, resplendent in feathered headdresses and embroidered loin-cloths came running from the jungle to surround her.

Patricia recognized these men immediately, not only from the descriptions she had had from Itzl Cha and Tarzan, but also because she had read a great deal concerning the civilization of the ancient Mayans. She was as familiar with their civilization, their religion, and their culture as the extensive research of many archaeological expeditions had been able to bring to light. It seemed to her that she had been suddenly carried back centuries to a long dead past, to which these little brown men belonged. She knew what her capture meant to her, for she knew the fate of Mayan prisoners. Her only hope lay in the possibility that the men of her party might be able to rescue her, and that hope was strong because of her faith in Tarzan.

"What are you going to do with me?" she said in the broken Mayan she had learned from Itzl Cha.

"That is for Cit Coh Xiu to decide," he said. "I shall send you back to Chichen Itza, back to the palace of the king"; then he instructed four of his warriors to take the prisoner to Cit Coh Xiu.

As Patricia was led away, Xatl Din and his remaining warriors continued on in the direction of Camp Saigon. The noble was quite pleased with himself. Even if he were not successful in bringing Itzl Cha back to Chichen Itza, he had at least furnished another sacrifice in her stead, and he would doubtless be praised by both the king and the high priest.

Colonel Leigh and his companions followed, quite by

accident, the same trail by which Patricia had come. They climbed the ledge which ran around the shoulder of the mountain; and, although badly winded, kept on almost at a run. Their advance was noisy and without caution, for their one thought was to find Patricia as quickly as possible; and when they were suddenly met by a band of plumed warriors, they were taken wholly by surprise. With savage war cries, the Mayans charged, hurling stones from their slings.

"Fire over their heads!" commanded the Colonel.

The terrifying noise momentarily stopped the Mayans, but when Xatl Din realized that it was only noise and that it had not injured any of his men, he ordered them to charge again; and once more their hideous war cries sounded in the ears of the whites.

"Shoot to kill!" snapped the Colonel; "we've got to stop those beggars before they reach us with their swords."

The rifles barked again, and four warriors fell. The others wavered, but Xatl Din urged them on.

These things that killed with a loud noise at a distance terrified the Mayans; and although some of them almost came to grips with the whites, they finally turned and fled, taking their wounded with them. Following their strategy, they scattered through the jungle so as to leave no well-marked trail to their city; and the whites, going in the wrong direction, became lost, for it is difficult to orient one's self in a dense jungle; and when they came to a steep declivity down a mountain side, they thought that they had crossed the mountain and were descending the opposite slope.

After stumbling about in dense shrubbery for an hour, they came suddenly to the end of the jungle, only to stand looking at one another in amazement, for before them lay the beach and their own camp.

"Well, I'll be damned!" ejaculated the Colonel.

As they approached the camp, Tibbett came to meet them, a troubled look on his face.

"Something wrong, Tibbet?" demanded the Colonel.

"I'll say there's something wrong, sir. I just came back from the Saigon with a load of planks to find that Schmidt and his outfit have stolen all the firearms and ammunition that were left in camp, as well as a considerable part of our stores."

"The scoundrels!" ejaculated the Colonel.

"But that's not the worst of it," continued Tibbet; "they took Miss Laon away with them."

De Groote went white. "Which way did they go, Tibbet?" he asked.

"Back up the beach," replied the second mate; "probably to their old camp."

De Groote, heartbroken and furious, started away. "Wait," said the Colonel; "where are you going?"

"I'm going after them," he said.

"They are all heavily armed," said the Colonel; "you couldn't do anything alone, and we can't spare men to go with you now—that is, we couldn't all go and leave Mrs. Leigh alone here again, with the chance that those painted devils may attack the camp at any time."

"I'm going anyway," said de Groote doggedly.

"I'll go with you," said Tibbet, and then two of the sailors from the Naiad also volunteered.

"I wish you luck," said the Colonel, "but for heaven's sake be careful. You'd better sneak up on the camp from the jungle side and snipe them from the concealment of the underbrush."

"Yes, sir," replied de Groote, as he and the three who had volunteered to accompany him started up the beach at a dog-trot.

## XXII

From a distance, Tarzan heard the firing during the encounter between the whites and the Mayans, and immediately turned and started back in the direction from which he thought the sounds came; but because of the echoes and reverberations caused by the mountains, he failed to locate it correctly, and went in the wrong direction. Also, he was misled by his assumption that any fighting there might be, would naturally be around Camp Saigon or Schmidt's camp.

Knowing that he was nearer Schmidt's camp then Camp Saigon, he decided to go there first and follow along the beach to Camp Saigon, if the fight were not at the former place.

As he approached the end of the forest opposite Schmidt's camp, he went more slowly and carefully, and it was well that he did for as he came in view of the camp, he saw the men returning and that the four whites were heavily armed. He saw Janette Laon being dragged along by Krause, and the Lascars bearing loads. He knew what had happened; but how it had happened, he could not guess. He naturally assumed that the shooting he had heard had marked an engagement between these men and those at Camp Saigon, and the inference was that Schmidt's party had been victorious. Perhaps all the other whites had been killed, but where was Patricia? Where was little Itzl Cha? He was not concerned over the fate of Penelope Leigh.

The Colonel was on the horns of a dilemma. The camp could boast of only four armed men now, scarcely enough to defend it; and he couldn't go out to search for Patricia and leave Penelope unguarded, nor could he divide his little force, for even four men would scarcely be enough to repel another attack by Schmidt or by the Mayans if they came in force, nor could four men hope successfully to storm the city of Chichen Itza to which he was convinced Patricia had been taken. And as the Colonel sought in vain for a solution of his problem, Patricia Leigh-Burden was led into the throne room of Cit Coh Xiu, King of Uxmal Island, and the leader of her escort addressed the king.

"The noble Xatl Din ordered us to bring this prisoner to his King and Master, as Xatl Din and his warriors continued on to attack the camp of the strangers. There was a battle, for we heard the strange noises with which these white men kill, but how the battle went we do not know."

The king nodded. "Xatl Din has done well," he said.

"He has done excellently," said Chal Yip Xiu, the high priest; "this woman will make a fitting offering to our gods."

Cit Coh Xiu's eyes appraised the white girl and found her beautiful. She was the first white woman that he had ever seen, and it suddenly occurred to him that it would be a shame to give her to some god that might not want her. He didn't dare say so aloud, but he thought that the girl was far too beautiful for any god; and, as a matter of fact, by the standards of any race, Patricia Leigh-Burden was beautiful.

"I think," said the king, "that I shall keep her as one of my handmaidens for a while."

Chal Yip Xiu, the high priest, looked at the king in well-simulated surprise. As a matter of fact, he was not surprised at all, for he knew his king, who had already robbed the gods of several pulchritudinous offerings. "If she is chosen for the gods," he said, "the gods will be angry with Cit Coh Xiu if he keeps her for himself."

"Perhaps it would be well," said the king, "if you were to see that she is not chosen—at least immediately. I don't think the gods want her anyway," he added.

Patricia, listening intently, had been able to understand at least the gist of this conversation. "A god has already chosen me," she said, "and he will be angry if you harm me."

Cit Coh Xiu looked at her in surprise. "She speaks the language of the Maya," he said to the high priest.

"But not very well," commented Chal Yip Xiu.

"The gods speak their own language," said Patricia; "they have little use for the language of mortals."

"Can it be that she is a goddess?" demanded the king.

"I am the mate of Che, Lord Forest," said Patricia. "He is already very angry with you for the way you treated him when he came to Chichen Itza. If you are wise, you will send me back to him. If you don't, he will certainly destroy you."

The king scratched his head and looked at his high priest questioningly. "Well," he said, "you should know all about gods, Chal Yip Xiu; was it indeed Che, Lord Forest, who came to Chichen Itza? Was it a god that you put in a wooden cage? Was it a god who stole the offering from the sacrificial altar?"

"It was not," snapped the high priest; "he was only a mortal."

"Nevertheless, we must not act hastily," said the king. "You may keep the girl temporarily; have her taken to the Temple of the Virgins, and see that she is well treated;" so Chal Yip Xiu summoned two lesser priests and told them to conduct the prisoner to The Temple of the Virgins.

Patricia felt that while she had not made much of an impression on the high priest, she had upon the king, and that at least she had won a reprieve which might give Tarzan and the others time in which to rescue her; and as she was lead from the Palace, her mind was sufficiently at ease to permit her to note the wonders of Chichen Itza.

Before her loomed a mighty pyramid of lava blocks, and up the steep stairs on one side of this, she was led to an ornately carved temple at the summit—The Temple of the Virgins. Here she was turned over to the high priestess who was in charge of the temple, in which were housed some fifty girls, mostly of noble families; for it was considered an honor to volunteer for this service. They kept the sacred fires alight and swept the temple floors. When they wished to, they might resign and marry; and they were always sought after by warriors and nobles.

Patricia stood in the temple colonnade and looked out over the city of Chichen Itza. She could see its palaces and temples clustered about the foot of the pyramid and the thatched huts of the common people beyond the wall, and beyond these the fields which extended to the edge of the jungle; and she fancied that she had been carried back many centuries to ancient Yucatan.

As Tarzan watched through the concealing verdure of the forest, he realized the futility of attempting to come out in the open and face four heavily armed men, while he was armed with only a bow. But Tarzan had ways of his own, and he was quite secure in the belief that he could take Janette away from these men without unnecessarily risking his own life.

He waited until they had come closer and the Lascars had thrown down their loads; then he fitted an arrow to his bow, and bending the latter until the point of the arrow rested against his left thumb, he took careful aim. The bow string twanged; and, an instant later, Krause screamed and pitched forward upon his face, an arrow through his heart.

The others looked about in consternation. "What happened" demanded Oubanovitch; "what's the matter with Krause?"

"He's dead," said Schmidt; "someone shot him with an arrow."

"The ape man," said Abdullah Abu Néjm; "who else could have done it?"

"Where is he?" demanded Schmidt.

"Here I am," said Tarzan, "and I have plenty more arrows. Come straight toward my voice, Janette, and into the forest; and if anyone tries to stop you, he'll get what Krause got."

Janette walked quickly toward the forest, and no hand was raised to detain her.

"That damn wildman!" ejaculated Schmidt, and then he broke into a volley of lurid profanity. "I'll get him!" I'll get him!" he screamed, and, raising his rifle, fired into the forest in the direction from which Tarzan's voice had come.

Again the bow-string twanged; and Schmidt, clutching at an arrow in his chest, dropped to his knees and then rolled over on his side, just as Janette entered the forest, and Tarzan dropped to the ground beside her.

"What happened at the camp?" he asked, and she told him briefly.

"So they let Schmidt and his gang come back," said Tarzan. "I am surprised at the Colonel."

"It was mostly the fault of that horrid old woman," said Janette.

"Come," said Tarzan, "we'll get back there as quickly as we can," and swinging Janette to his shoulder, he took to the trees. As he and Janette approached Camp Saigon, de Groote, Tibbet, and the two sailors came into sight of Schmidt's camp.

A quick glance around the camp did not reveal Janette, but de Groote saw two men lying on the ground, and the Lascars huddled to one side, apparently terrified.

Abdullah was the first to see de Groote and his party, and knowing that they had come for revenge and would show no quarter, he swung his rifle to his shoulder and fired. He missed, and de Groote and Tibbet ran forward, firing, the two sailors, armed only with gaffs, at their heels.

Several shots were exchanged without any casualties, and then de Groote dropped to one knee and took careful aim, and Tibbet followed his example. "Take Oubanovitch," said de Groote; "I'll get the Arab."

The two rifles spoke almost simultaneously, and Oubanovitch and Abdullah Abu Néjm dropped in their tracks.

De Groote and Tibbet ran forward, followed by the sailors, ready to finish off any of the men who still showed fight; but the Russian, the Arab, and Krause were dead, and Schmidt was writhing and screaming in agony, helpless to harm them.

De Groote bent over him. "Where is Miss Laon?" he demanded.

Screaming and cursing, his words almost unintelligible, Schmidt mumbled, "The wildman, damn him, he took her;" and then he died.

"Thank God!" ejaculated de Groote; "she's safe now."

The four took the arms and ammunition from the bodies of the dead men, and with the authority which they gave them, forced the Lascars to pick up their packs and start back toward Camp Saigon.

## XXIII

As Tarzan and Janette stepped from the jungle and approached the camp, they were greeted by a disheartened and hopeless company, only one of whom found anything to be thankful for. It was Penelope Leigh. When she saw them, she said to Algy, "At least Patricia was not with that creature."

"Oh, come now, Aunt Pen," said Algy impatiently; "I suppose you will say now that Tarzan and Janette arranged all this so that they could meet in the jungle."

"I should not have been at all surprised," replied Mrs. Leigh. "A man who would carry on with an Indian girl might do anything."

Tarzan was disgusted with all that had been happening during his absence, largely because his orders had been disobeyed, but he only said, "They should never have been permitted within pistol shot of this camp."

"It was my fault," said Colonel Leigh; "I did it against my better judgment, because it did seem inhuman to send them back there unarmed, with a man-eater hanging around their camp."

"It was not the Colonel's fault," said Janette, furiously; "he was nagged into it. That hateful old woman is most to blame. She insisted; and now, because of her, Hans may be killed." Even as she ceased speaking, they heard the distant reports of firearms, coming faintly from the direction of Schmidt's camp. "There!" cried Janette; then she turned on Mrs. Leigh: "If anything happens to Hans, his blood is on your head!" she cried.

"What has been done has been done," said Tarzan; "the important thing now, is to find Patricia. Are you positive that she was captured by the Maya?"

"We heard two shots," explained the Colonel, "and when we went to investigate, we were met by fully a hundred Maya warriors. We dispersed them, but were unable to follow their trail; and although we saw nothing of Patricia, it seems most probable that she had been captured by them before we met them."

"And now, William, I hope you are satisfied," said Mrs. Leigh; "it is all your fault, for coming on that silly expedition in the first place."

"Yes, Penelope," said the Colonel resignedly, "I suppose that it is all my fault, but telling me that over and over again doesn't help matters any."

Tarzan took Itzl Cha aside to talk to her away from the interruptions of the others. "Tell me, Itzl Cha," he said, "what your people would probably do with Patricia."

"Nothing, two, three days, maybe month," replied the girl; "then they offer her to a god."

"Look at that creature now," said Penelope Leigh, "taking that little Indian girl off and whispering to her. I can well imagine what he is saying."

"Would they put Patricia in the cage where they had me?" Tarzan asked.

"I think in The Temple of the Virgins at the top of the sacred pyramid; Temple of the Virgins very sacred place and well guarded."

"I can reach it," said Tarzan.

"You are not going there?" demanded Itzl Cha.

"Tonight," said Tarzan.

The girl threw her arms about him. "Please don't go," she begged; "you cannot save her, and they will kill you."

"Look!" exclaimed Penelope Leigh; "of all the brazen things I've ever seen in my life! William, you must put a stop to it. I cannot stand it; I have never before had to associate with loose people," and she cast a venomous glance at Janette.

Tarzan disengaged the girl's arms. "Come, come, Itzl Cha," he said; "I shall not be killed."

"Don't go," she pleaded. "Oh, Che, Lord Forest, I love you. Take me away into the forest with you. I do not like these people."

"They have been very kind to you," Tarzan reminded her.

"I know," said Itzl Cha sullenly, "but I do not want their kindness; I want only you, and you must not go to Chichen Itza tonight nor ever."

Tarzan smiled and patted her shoulder. "I go tonight," he said.

"You love her," cried Itzl Cha; "that is the reason you are going. You are leaving me for her."

"That will be all," said Tarzan firmly; "say no more"; then he left her and joined the others, and Cha, furious with jealously, went into her hut and threw herself upon the ground, kicking it with her sandaled feet and beating it with her little fists. Presently she arose and looked out through the doorway, just in time to see de Groote and his party returning, and while the attention of all the others was centered upon them, little Itzl Cha crept from her hut and ran into the jungle.

Janette ran forward and threw her arms about de Groote, tears of joy running down her cheeks. "I thought that you had been killed, Hans," she sobbed; "I thought that you had been killed."

"I am very much alive," he said, "and you have nothing more to fear from Schmidt and his gang; they are all dead."

"I am glad," said Tarzan; "they were bad men."

Little Itzl Cha ran through the jungle. She was terrified, for it was growing dark, and there are demons and the spirits of the dead in the forest at night; but she ran on, spurred by jealousy and hate and desire for revenge.

She reached Chichen Itza after dark, and the guard at the gate was not going to admit her until she told him who she was, and that she had important word for Chal Yip Xiu, the high priest. She was taken to him then, and she fell on her knees before him.

"Who are you?" he demanded, and then he recognized her. "So you have come back," he said. "Why?"

"I came to tell you that the man who stole me from the sacrificial altar is coming tonight to take the white girl from the temple."

"For this you deserve much from the gods," said Chal Yip Xiu, "and again you shall be honored by being offered to them," and little Itzl Cha was placed in a wooden cage to await sacrifice.

Tarzan came slowly through the forest on his way to

Chichen Itza. He did not wish to arrive before midnight, when he thought that the city would have quieted down and most of its inmates would be asleep. A gentle wind was blowing in his face, and it brought to his nostrils a familiar scent spoor—Tantor, the elephant, was abroad. He had found an easier trail to the plateau than the shorter one which Tarzan used, and he had also found on the plateau a plenteous supply of the tender shoots he loved best.

Tarzan did not call him until he had come quite close, and then he spoke in a low voice; and Tantor, recognizing his voice, came and verified his judgment by passing his trunk over the ape man's body.

At a word of command, he lifted Tarzan to his withers, and the Lord of the Jungle rode to the edge of the forest just outside of the city of Chichen Itza.

Slipping from Tantor's head, Tarzan crossed the fields to the city wall. Before he reached it, he broke into a run, and when it loomed before him, he scaled it much as a cat would have done. The city was quiet and the streets were deserted; so that Tarzan reached the foot of the pyramid without encountering anyone.

Just inside the entrance to The Temple of the Virgins, a dozen warriors hid in the shadows as Tarzan climbed the steps to the summit. Outside the temple he stopped and listened; then he walked around to the lee side, so that the breeze that was blowing would carry to his sensitive nostrils the information that he wished.

He stood there for a moment; and then, satisfied, he crept stealthily around to the entrance. At the threshold he stopped again and listened; then he stepped inside, and as he did so a net was thrown over him and drawn tight, and a dozen warriors fell upon him and so entangled him in the meshes that he was helpless.

A priest stepped from the temple and raising a trumpet to his lips, blew three long blasts. As by magic, the city awoke, lights appeared, and people came streaming towards the temple pyramid.

Tarzan was carried down the long flight of steps, and at the bottom, he was surrounded by priests in long embroidered cloaks and gorgeous headdresses. Then they brought

114

Patricia. With trumpets and drums preceding them, Cit Coh Xiu, the king, and Chal Yip Xiu, the high priest, headed a procession that wound through the city and out of the east gate.

Tarzan had been placed on a litter that was carried by four priests; behind him walked Patricia, under guard; and behind her little Itzl Cha was carried in her wooden cage. A full moon cast its soft light on the barbaric procession, which was further illuminated by hundreds of torches carried by the marchers.

The procession wound through the forest to the foot of a mountain, up which it zig-zagged back and forth until it reached the rim of the crater of an extinct volcano at the summit. It was almost dawn as the procession made its way down a narrow trail to the bottom of the crater and stopped there at the edge of a yawning hole. Priests intoned a chant to the accompaniment of flutes, drums, and trumpets; and, just at dawn, the bag was cut away from Tarzan and he was hurled into the chasm, notwithstanding the pleas of Itzl Cha, who had repented and warned the priests that the man was really Che, Lord Forest. She had begged them not to kill him, but Chal Yip Xiu had silenced her and spoken the word that sent Tarzan to his doom.

# XXIV

Patricia Leigh-Burden was not the type of girl easily moved to tears, but she stood now on the brink of that terrible abyss, her body racked by sobs; and then as the sun topped the rim and shed its light down into the crater, she saw Tarzan swimming slowly about in a pond some seventy feet below her. Instantly her mind leaped to the stories she had read of the sacred dzonot of ancient Chichen Itza in Yucatan, and hope burned again in her breast.

"Tarzan," she called, and the man turned over on his back and looked up at her. "Listen," she continued. "I know this form of sacrifice well; it was practiced by the Maya in Central America hundreds and hundreds of years ago. The victim was thrown into the sacred well at Chichen Itza at dawn, and if he still lived at noon, he was taken out and raised to highest rank; he became practically a living god on earth. You must keep afloat until noon, Tarzan; you must! you must!"

Tarzan smiled up at her and waved. The priests eyed her suspiciously, though they had no idea what she had said to their victim.

"Do you think that you can, Tarzan?" she said. "You must, because I love you."

Tarzan did not reply, as he turned over and commenced to swim slowly around the pool, which was about a hundred feet in diameter with perpendicular sides of smooth volcanic glass.

The water was chilly but not cold, and Tarzan swam just strongly enough to keep from becoming chilled.

The people had brought food and drink; and as they watched through the long dragging hours, they made a fiesta of the occasion.

As the sun climbed toward zenith, Chal Yip Xiu commenced to show signs of strain and nervousness, for if the victim lived until noon, he might prove indeed to be Che, Lord Forest, which would be most embarrassing for the ah kin mai. Every eye that could see it was upon a crude sun-dial that stood beside the rim of the dzonot; and when it marked noon, a great shout arose, for the victim was still alive.

The high priest was furious as the people acclaimed Tarzan as Che, Lord Forest, and demanded that he be taken from the water. A long rope was thrown down to him, with a noose in the end of it by means of which he could be drawn out of the dzonot; but Tarzan ignored the noose and clambered up the rope, hand over hand. When he stepped out upon the rim, the people fell to their knees before him and sup-plicated him for forgiveness and for favors.

The king and the high priest looked most uncomfortable as Tarzan faced them. "I came to earth in the form of a mortal," he said, "to see how you ruled my people of Chichen Itza. I am not pleased. I shall come again some day to see if you have improved. Now I go, and I take this woman with me," and he placed a hand upon Patricia's arm. "I command you to release Itzl Cha, and to see that neither she nor any others are sacrificed before I return."

He took Patricia by the hand, and together they climbed the steep trail to the rim of the crater and then down the side of the volcano, the people following them, in a long proces-sion, singing as they marched. As they reached the city, Tarzan turned and held up a hand. "Come no farther," he said to the people, and then to Patricia, "Now I'll give them something to tell their grandchildren about."

She looked up at him questioningly and smiled. "What are you going to do?" she asked.

For answer, he voiced a long weird cry, and then, in the language of the great apes, shouted, "Come, Tantor, come!" and as he and Patricia crossed the field and approached the forest, a great bull elephant came out of it to meet them, and a cry of astonishment and fear rose from the people behind them.

"Won't he gore us or something?" asked Patricia, as they approached the bull.

"He is my friend," said Tarzan, laying his hand upon the trunk of the great beast. "Don't be frightened," he said

117

to Patricia; "he is going to lift you to his withers," and at a word of command, Tantor swung the girl up and then lifted Tarzan.

As he wheeled to go into the forest, Tarzan and Patricia looked back to see the people of Chichen Itza all kneeling, their faces pressed against the ground.

"Their great-great-grandchildren will hear of this," said Patricia.

In Camp Saigon, the discouraged company waited hopelessly for Tarzan's return. There had been little sleep the previous night for many of them, and the long hours of the morning had dragged heavily. Tea time came and Tarzan had not returned; but, as a matter of habit, they had tea served; and as they sat around the table, sipping it listlessly, the same thought must have been in the minds of all; they would never see Patricia or Tarzan again.

"You should never have let that creature go out after Patricia alone," said Mrs. Leigh; "he probably found her all right, and there is no telling what has happened to her by this time."

"Oh, Penelope!" cried the Colonel hopelessly. "Why are you so bitter against that man? He has done nothing but befriend us."

"Hmph!" exclaimed Penelope. "You are very dense, William; I could see through him from the first—he is a climber; he wants to get into our good graces and then he will probably try to marry Patricia for the money she will inherit."

"Madam," said de Groote very icily, "'that creature,' as you call him, is John Clayton, Lord Greystoke, an English viscount."

"Bosh!" exclaimed Mrs. Leigh.

"It is not bosh," said de Groote; "Krause told me who he was while we were locked up together in that cage. He got it from the Arab, who has known the man for years."

Mrs. Leigh's chin dropped, and she seemed to suddenly deflate, but she rallied quickly. "I rather expected it," she said after a moment. "All that I ever criticized in him was his predilection for nudity. Why didn't you ever tell us this before, young man?"

"I don't know why I told you now," replied de Groote; "it is none of my business; if he had wanted us to know, he would have told us."

"Here he comes now!" exclaimed Janette, "and Patricia is with him!"

"How wonderful!" exclaimed Penelope. "What a fine looking couple my niece and Lord Greystoke make."

From the withers of the elephant, Patricia could see far out beyond the reef; and when she and Tarzan slipped to the ground, she ran toward the group awaiting them, pointing and crying, "Look! A ship! A ship!"

It was a ship far out; and the men hastened to build a fire on the beach, and when it was burning, to throw on green leaves and kerosene until a great black smoke rose high into the sky.

De Groote and some of the sailors put out in one of the boats in a frantic, if potentially futile, effort to further attract the ship's attention.

"They don't see us," said Janette.

"And there may not be another ship in a hundred years," remarked Dr. Crouch.

"Jolly long time to wait for anything, what?" said Algy.

"They've changed their course," said Bolton; "they're heading in."

The Colonel had gone to his hut and now he came out with binoculars in his hand. He took a long look through them; and when he took the glasses down, there were tears in his eyes; and it was a moment before he could speak.

"It's the Naiad," he said, "and she *is* heading inshore."

That night, under a full tropic moon, two couples lounged in comfortable chairs on the deck of the Naiad. Tarzan laid a hand on one of Patricia's. "In your nervous excitement today at the Dzonot, you said something, Patricia, that we must both forget."

"I know what you mean," she replied. "You see, I didn't know then that it was impossible—but I meant it then, and I shall always mean it."

"Tarzan!" called de Groote from the other side of the

yacht. "Janette is trying to convince me that the Captain can't marry us. She's wrong, isn't she?"

"I am quite sure that she is wrong," replied the ape man.

# TARZAN
# AND
# THE CHAMPION

\*

\*

\*

\*

\*

\*

"Six—seven—eight—nine—*ten!*" The referee stepped to a neutral corner and hoisted Mullargan's right hand "The winnah and new champion!" he shouted.

For a moment the audience, which only partially filled Madison Square Garden, sat in stunned and stupefied silence; then there was a burst of applause, intermingled with which was an almost equal volume of boos. It wasn't that the booers questioned the correctness of the decision—they just didn't like Mullargan, a notoriously dirty fighter. Doubtless, too, many of them had had their dough on the champion.

Joey Marks, Mullargan's manager, and the other man who had been in his corner crawled through the ropes and slapped Mullargan on the back; photographers, sportswriters, police, and a part of the audience converged on the ring; jittery news-commentators bawled the epochal tidings to a waiting world.

The former champion, revived but a bit wobbly, crossed the ring and proffered a congratulatory hand to Mullargan. The new champion did not take the hand. "Gwan, you bum," he said, and turned his back. . . .

"One-Punch" Mullargan had come a long way in a little more than a year—from amateur to preliminary fighter, to

Heavyweight Champion of the World; and he had earned his sobriquet. He had, in truth, but one punch; and he needed but that one—a lethal right to the button. Sometimes he had had to wait several rounds before he found an opening, but eventually he had always found it. The former champion, a ten-to-one favorite at ringside, had gone down in the third round. Since then, One-Punch Mullargan had fought but nine rounds; yet he had successfully defended his championship six times, leaving three men with broken jaws and one with a fractured skull. After all, who wishes his skull fractured?

So One-Punch Mullargan decided to take a vacation and do something he always had wanted to do but which fate had always heretofore intervened to prevent. Several years before, he had seen a poster which read, "JOIN THE NAVY AND SEE THE WORLD;" he had always remembered that poster; and now, with a vacation on his hands, Mullargan decided to go and see the world for himself, without any assistance from Navy or Marines.

"I aint never seen Niag'ra Falls," said his manager. "That would be a nice place to go for a vacation. If we was to go there, that would give Niag'ra Falls a lot of publicity too."

"Niag'ra Falls, my foot!" said Mullargan. "We're goin' to Africa."

"Africa," mused Mr. Marks. "That's a hell of a long ways off—down in South America somewheres. Wot you wanna go there for?"

"Huntin'. You see them heads in that guy's house what we were at after the fight the other night, didn't you? Lions, buffaloes, elephants. Gee! That must be some sport."

"We ain't lost no lions, kid," said Marks. There was a note of pleading in his voice. "Listen, kid: stick around here for a couple more fights; then you'll have enough potatoes to retire on, and you can go to Africa or any place you want to —but not me."

"I'm goin' to Africa, and you're goin' with me. If you want to get some publicity out of it, you better call up them newspaper bums."

Sports-writers and camera-men milled about the champion on the deck of the ship ten days later. Bulbs flashed; shutters clicked; reporters shot questions; passengers crowded

122

closer with craning necks; a girl elbowed her way through the throng with an autograph album.

"When did *he* learn to write?" demanded a Daily *News* man.

"Wise guy," growled Mullargan.

"Give my love to Tarzan when you get to Africa," said another.

"And don't get fresh with him, or he'll take you apart," interjected the Daily *News* man.

"I seen that bum in pitchers," said Mullargan. "He couldn't take nobody apart."

"I'll lay you ten to one he could K.O. you in the first round," taunted the Daily *News* man.

"You aint got ten, you bum," retorted the champion.

A heavily laden truck lumbered along the edge of a vast plain under the guns of the forest which had halted here, sending out a scattering of pickets to reconnoiter the terrain held by the enemy. Why the tree army never advanced, why the plain always held its own—these are mysteries.

And the lorry was a mystery to the man far out on the plain, who watched its slow advance. He knew that there were no tracks there, that perhaps since creation this was the first wheeled vehicle that had ever passed this way.

A white man in a disreputable sun-helmet drove the truck; beside him sat a black man; sprawled on top of the load were several other blacks. The lengthening shadow of the forest stretched far beyond the crawling anachronism, marking the approach of the brief equatorial twilight.

The man out upon the plain set his course so that he might meet the truck. He moved with an easy, sinuous stride that was almost catlike in its smoothness. He wore no clothes other than a loin-cloth; his weapons were primitive: a quiver of arrows and a bow at his back, a hunting-knife in a rude scabbard at his hip, a short, stout spear that he carried in his hand. Looped across one shoulder and beneath the opposite arm was a coil of grass rope. The man was very dark, but he was not a Negro. A lifetime beneath the African sun accounted for his bronzed skin.

Upon his shoulder squatted a little monkey, one arm around

the bronzed neck. *"Tarmangani,* Nkima," said the man, looking in the direction of the truck.

*"Tarmangani,"* chattered the monkey. "Nkima and Tarzan will kill the *tarmangani."* He stood up and blew out his cheeks and looked very ferocious. At a great distance from an enemy, or when upon the shoulder of his master, little Nkima was a lion at heart. His courage was in inverse ratio to the distance that separated him from Tarzan, and in direct ratio to that which lay between himself and danger. If little Nkima had been a man, he would probably have been a gangster and certainly a bully; but he still would have been a coward. Being just a little monkey, he was only amusing. He did, however, possess one characteristic which, upon occasion, elevated him almost to heights of sublimity. That was his self-sacrificing loyalty to his master, Tarzan.

At last the man on the truck saw the man on foot, saw that they were going to meet a little farther on. He shifted his pistol to a more accessible position and loosened it in its holster. He glanced at the rifle that the boy beside him was holding between his knees, and saw that it was within easy reach. He had never been in this locality before, and did not know the temper of the natives. It was well to take precautions. As the distance between them lessened, he sought to identify the stranger.

*"Mtu mweusi?"* he inquired of the boy beside him, who was also watching the approaching stranger.

*"Mzungu, bwana,"* replied the boy.

"I guess you're right," agreed the man. "I guess he's a white man, all right, but he's sure dressed up like a native."

*"Menyi wazimo,"* laughed the boy.

"I got two crazy men on my hands now," said the man. "I don't want another." He brought the truck to a stop as Tarzan approached.

Little Nkima was chattering and scolding fiercely, baring his teeth in what he undoubtedly thought was a terrifying snarl. Nobody paid any attention to him, but he held his ground until Tarzan was within fifty feet of the truck; then he leaped to the ground and sought the safety of a tree near by. After all, what was the use of tempting fate?

Tarzan stopped beside the truck and looked up into the white man's face. "What are you doing here?" he asked.

Melton, looking down upon an almost naked man, felt his own superiority; and resented the impertinence of the query. Incidentally, he had noted that the stranger carried no firearms.

"I'm drivin' a lorry, buddy," he said.

"Answer my question." This time Tarzan's tone had an edge to it.

Melton had had a hard day. As a matter of fact, he had had a number of hard days. He was worried, and his nerves were on edge. His hand moved to the butt of his pistol as he formulated a caustic rejoinder, but he never voiced it. Tarzan's arm shot out; his hand seized Melton's wrist and dragged the man from the cab of the truck. An instant later he was disarmed.

Nkima danced up and down upon the branch of his tree and hurled jungle billingsgate at the enemy, intermittently screaming at Tarzan to kill the *tarmangani*. No one paid any attention to him. That was a cross that Nkima always had to bear. He was so little and insignificant that no one ever paid any attention to him.

The blacks on the truck sat in wide-eyed confusion. The thing had happened so suddenly that it had caught their wits off guard. They saw the stranger dragging Melton away from the truck, shaking him as a dog shakes a rat. Tarzan had learned from experience that there is no surer way of reducing a man to subservience than by shaking him. Perhaps he knew nothing of the psychology of the truth, but he knew the truth.

The latter was a powerful man, but he was helpless in the grip of the stranger; and he was frightened, too. There was something more terrifying about this creature than his superhuman strength. There was the quite definite sensation of being in the clutches of a wild beast, so that his reactions were much the same as they had been many years before when he had been mauled by a lion—something of a fatalistic resignation to the inevitable.

Tarzan stopped shaking Melton and turned his eyes on the

125

boy with the rifle, who had jumped down from the truck. "Throw down the rifle," he said in Swahili.

The boy hesitated. "Throw it down," ordered Melton; and then, to Tarzan: "What do you want of me?"

"I asked you what you were doing here. I want an answer."

"I'm guidin' a couple of bloomin' Yanks."

"Where are they?"

Melton shrugged. "Gawd only knows. They started out early this morning in a light car, and told me to keep along the edge of the forest. Said they'd come back an' meet me later in the day. They're probably lost. They're both balmy."

"What are they doing here?" asked Tarzan.

"Hunting."

"Why did you bring them here? This is closed territory."

"I didn't bring 'em here; they brought me. You can't tell Mullargan nothing. He's one of those birds that knows it all. He don't need a guide; what he needs is a keeper. He's Heavyweight Champion of the World, and it's gone to his head. Try to tell him anything, and he's just as likely as not to slap you down. He's knocked the boys around something awful. I never saw such a rotten bounder in my life. The other one aint so bad. He's Mullargan's manager. That's a laugh. Manager, my eye! All he says is, 'Yes, kid!' 'Okay, kid!' and all he wants to do is get back to New York. He's scared to death all the time. I wish to hell they was both back in New York. I wish I was rid of 'em."

"Are they out alone?" asked Tarzan.

"Yes."

"Then you may be rid of them. This is lion country. I have never seen them so bad."

Melton whistled. "Then I got to push on and try to find 'em. I don't like 'em, but I'm responsible for 'em. You"— he hesitated—"you aint goin' to try to stop me, are you?"

"No," said Tarzan. "Go and find them, and tell them to get out of this country and stay out." Then he started on toward the forest.

When he had gone a short distance, Melton called to him. "Who are you, anyway?" he demanded.

The ape-man paused and turned around. "I am Tarzan," he said.

Again Melton whistled. He climbed back into the cab of the truck and started the motor; and as the heavy vehicle got slowly under way, Tarzan disappeared into the forest.

The sun swung low into the west, and the lengthening shadow of the forest stretched far out into the plain. A light car bounced and jumped over the uneven ground. There were two men in the car. One of them drove, and the other braced himself and held on. His eyes were red-rimmed; he sneezed almost continuously.

"Fer cripe's sake, kid, can't you slow down?" wailed Marks. "Aint this hayfever bad enough without you tryin' to jounce the liver out of me?"

For answer Mullargan pressed the accelerator down a little farther.

"You won't have no springs or no tires or no manager, if you don't slow down."

"I don't need no manager no more." That struck Mullargan as being so funny that he repeated it. "I don't need no manager no more; so I bounces him out in Africa. Gee, wouldn't dat give the guys a laugh!"

"Don't get no foolish ideas in your head, kid. You need a smart fella like me, all right. All you got is below them big cauliflower ears of yours."

"Is zat so?"

"Yes, zat's so."

Mullargan slowed down a little, for it had suddenly grown dark. He switched on the lights. "It sure gets dark in a hurry here," he commented. "I wonder why."

"It's the altitude, you dope," explained Marks.

They rode on in silence for a while. Marks glanced nervously to right and left, for with the coming of night, the entire aspect of the scene had changed as though they had been suddenly tossed into a strange world. The plain was dimly lined in the ghostly light of pale stars; the forest was solid, impenetrable blackness.

"Forty-second Street would look pretty swell right now," observed Marks.

"So would some grub," said Mullargan; "my belly's wrapped around my backbone. I wonder what became of that so-an'-so.

I told him to keep right on till he met us. Them English is too damn' cocky—think they know it all, tellin' me not to do this an' not to do that. I guess the Champeen of the World can take care of himself, all right."

"You said it, kid."

The silence of the plain was broken by the grunting of a hunting lion. It was still some distance away, but the sound came plainly to the ears of the two men.

"What was that?" queried Mullargan.

"A pig," said Marks.

"If it was daylight, we might get a shot at it," observed Mullargan. "A bunch of pork chops wouldn't go so bad right now. You know, Joey, I been thinkin' me and you could get along all right without that English so-an'-so."

"Who'd drive the truck?"

"That's so," admitted Mullargan; "but he's got to stop treatin' us like we was a couple o' kids and he was our nurse-girl. Pretty soon I'm goin' to get sore and hand him one."

"Look!" exclaimed Marks. "There's a light—it must be the truck."

When the two cars met, the tired men dropped to the ground and stretched stiffened limbs and cramped muscles.

"Where you been?" demanded Mullargan.

"Coming right along ever since we broke camp," replied Melton. "You know this bus can't cover the ground like that light car of yours, and you must have covered a lot of it today. Any luck?"

"No. I don't believe there's any game around here."

"There's plenty. If you'll make a permanent camp somewhere, as I've been telling you, we'll get something."

"We seen some buffaloes today," said Marks, "but they got away."

"They went into some woods," explained Mullargan. "I followed 'em in on foot, but they got away."

"Lucky for you they did," observed Melton.

"What you mean—lucky for me?"

"If you'd shot one of 'em, you'd probably have been killed. I'd rather face a lion any day than a wounded buffalo."

"Maybe you would," said Mullargan, "but I aint afraid of no cow."

Melton shrugged, turned and set the boys to making camp. "We've got to camp where we are," he said to the other two whites. "We couldn't find water now; and we've got enough anyway, such as it is. Anyway, tomorrow we must turn back."

"Turn back?" exclaimed Mullargan. "Who says we gotta turn back? I come here to hunt, an' I'm goin' to hunt."

"I met a man back there a way who says this is closed territory. He told me we'd have to get out."

"Oh, he did, did he? Who the hell does he think he is, tellin' me to get out? Did you tell him who I was?"

"Yes, but he didn't seem to be much impressed."

"Well, I'll impress him if I see him. Who was he?"

"His name is Tarzan."

"Dat bum? Does he think he can run me out of Africa?"

"If he tells you to leave this part of Africa, you'd better," Melton advised.

"I'll leave when I get good an' damn' ready," said Mullargan.

"I'm ready to go right now," said Marks, between sneezes. "This here Africa aint no place for a guy with hayfever."

The boys were unloading the truck, hurrying to make camp. One was building a fire preparatory to cooking supper. There was much laughter, and now and then a snatch of native song. One of the boys, carrying a heavy load from the truck, accidentally bumped into Mullargan and threw him off balance. The fighter swung a vicious blow at the black with his open palm, striking him across the side of his head and knocking him to the ground.

"You'll look where you're goin' next time," he growled.

Melton came up to him. "That'll be all of that," he said. "I've stood it as long as I'm goin' to. Don't ever hit another of these boys."

"So you're lookin' for it too, are you?" shouted Mullargan. "All right, you're goin' to get it."

Before he could strike, Melton drew his pistol and covered

him. "Come on," he invited. "I'm just waitin' for the chance to plead guilty to killin' you in self-defense."

Mullargan stood staring at the gun for several seconds; then he turned away. Later he confided to Marks: "Them English aint got no sense of humor. He might of seen I was just kiddin'."

The evening meal was a subdued affair. Conversation could not accurately have been said to lag, since it did not even exist until the meal was nearly over; then the grunting of a lion was heard close to the camp.

"There's that pig again," said Mullargan. "Maybe we can get him now."

"What pig?" asked Melton.

"You must be deaf," said Mullargan. "Can't you hear him?"

"Cripes!" exclaimed Marks. "Look at his eyes shine out there."

Melton rose and stepping to the side of the truck switched on the spotlight and swung it around upon the eyes. In the circle of bright light stood a full-grown lion. Just for a moment he stood there; then he turned and slunk off into the darkness.

"Pig!" said Mullargan, disgustedly.

A chocolate-colored people are the Babangos, with good features and well-shaped heads. Their teeth are not filed; yet they are inveterate man-eaters. There are no religious implications in their cannibalism, no superstitions. They eat human flesh because they like it, because they prefer it to any other food; and like true gourmets, they know how to prepare it. They hunt man as other men hunt game animals, and they are hated and feared throughout the territory that they raid.

Recently, word had been brought to Tarzan that the Babangos had invaded a remote portion of that vast domain which, from boyhood, he had considered his own; and Tarzan had come, making many marches, to investigate. Behind him, moving more slowly, came a band of his own white-plumed Waziri warriors, led by Muviro, their famous chief. . . .

It was the morning following Tarzan's encounter with Melton. The ape-man was swinging along just inside the forest at the edge of the plain, his every sense alert. There was no slightest suggestion of caution in his free stride and confident demeanor; yet he moved as silently as a shadow. He saw the puff adder in the grass and the python waiting in the tree to seize its prey from above, and he avoided them. He made a little detour, lest he pass beneath a trumpet tree from which black ants might drop upon and sting him.

Presently he halted and turned, looking back along the edge of the forest and the plain. Neither you nor I could have heard what he heard, because our lives have not depended to a great extent upon the keenness of our hearing. There are wild beasts which have notoriously poor eyesight, but none with poor hearing or a deficient sense of smell. Tarzan, being a man and therefore poorly equipped by nature to survive in his savage world, had developed all his senses to an extraordinary degree; and so it was that now he heard pounding hoofs in the far distance long before you or I could have. And he heard another sound—a sound as strange to that locale as would be the after-kill roar of a lion on Park Avenue: the exhaust of a motor.

They were coming closer now; and they were coming fast. And now there came another sound, drowning out the first— the staccato of a machine-gun. Presently they tore past him— a herd of zebra; and clinging to their flank was a light car. One man drove, and the other pumped lead from a sub-machine gun into the fleeing herd. Zebra fell, some killed, some only maimed; but the car sped on, its occupants ignoring the suffering beasts in its wake.

Tarzan, helpless to prevent it, viewed the slaughter in cold anger. He had witnessed the brutality of game-hogs before, but never anything like this. His estimate of man, never any too high, reached nadir. He went out into the plain and mercifully put out of their misery those of the animals which were hopelessly wounded, following the trail of destruction in the direction that the car had taken. Eventually he would come upon the two men again, and there would be an accounting.

Far ahead of him, the survivors of the terrified herd

plunged into a rock gully; and clambering up the opposite side, disappeared over the ridge as Mullargan brought the car to a stop near the bottom.

"Gee!" he exclaimed. "Was dat sport! When I gets all my heads up on a wall, I'll make that Park Avenue guy look like a piker."

"You sure cleaned 'em up, kid," said Marks. "That was some shootin'."

"I wasn't a expert rifleman in the Marine Corps for nothin', Joey. Now if I could just run into a flock of lions—boy!"

The forest came down into the head of the gorge, and the trees grew thickly to within a hundred yards of the car. There was a movement among the trees there, but neither of the dull-witted men were conscious of it. They had lighted cigars and were enjoying a few moments of relaxation.

"I guess we better start back an' mop up," said Mullargan. "I don't want to lose none of 'em. Say, at this rate I ought to take back about a thousand heads if we put in a full month. I'll sure give them newspaper bums somep'n to write about when I get home. I'll have one of them photographer bums take my pitcher settin' on top of a thousand heads—all kinds. That'll get in every newspaper in the U.S."

"It sure will, kid," agreed Marks. "We'll sure give Africa a lot of publicity." As he spoke, his eyes were on the forest up the gorge. Suddenly his brows knitted. "Say, kid, lookit! What's that?"

Mullargan looked, and then cautiously picked up the machine-gun. "S-s-sh!" he cautioned. "That's a elephant. What luck!" He raised the muzzle of the weapon and squeezed the trigger. An elephant trumpeted and lurched out into the open. It was followed by another and another, until seven of the great beasts were coming toward them; then the gun jammed.

"Hell!" exclaimed Mullargan. "They'll get away before I can clear this."

"They ain't goin' away," said Marks. "They're comin' for us."

The elephants, poor of eyesight, finally located the car. Their trunks and their great ears went up, as, trumpeting, they charged; but by that time Mullargan had cleared the

132

gun and was pouring lead into them again. One elephant went down. Others wavered and turned aside. It was too much for them—too much for all but one, a great bull, which, maddened by the pain of many wounds, carried the charge home.

The sound of the machine-gun ceased. Mullargan threw the weapon down in disgust. "Beat it, Joey!" he yelled; "the drum's empty."

The two men tumbled over the opposite side of the car as the bull struck it. The weight of the great body, the terrific impact, rolled the car over, wheels up. The bull staggered and lurched forward, falling across the chassis, dead.

The two men came slowly back. "Gee!" said Mullargan. "Look wot he went an' done to that jalopy! Henry wouldn't never recognize it now." He got down on his hands and knees and tried to peer underneath the wreck.

Marks was shaking like an aspen. "Suppose he hadn't of croaked," he said; "where would we of been? Wot we goin' to do now?"

"We gotta wait here until the truck comes. Our guns is all underneath that mess. Maybe the truck can drag the big bum off. We gotta have our guns."

"I wish to Gawd I was back on Broadway," said Marks, sneezing, "where there ain't no elephants or no hay."

Little Nkima was greatly annoyed. In the first place, the blast of the machine-gun had upset him. It had frightened him so badly that he had abandoned the sanctuary of his lord and master's shoulder and scampered to the uttermost pinnacle of a near-by tree. When Tarzan had gone out on the plain, he had followed; and he didn't like it at all out on the plain, because the fierce African sun beat down, and there was no protection. And he was further annoyed because he had continued to hear the nerve-shattering sound intermittently for quite some time, and it came from the direction in which they were going. As he scampered along behind, he scolded his master; for little Nkima saw no sense in looking for trouble in a world in which there was already more than enough looking for you.

Tarzan had heard the sound of the gunning, the squeals

133

of hurt elephants and the trumpeting of angry elephants; and he visualized the brutal tragedy as clearly as though he saw it with his eyes; and his anger rose so that he forgot the law of the white man, for Tantor the elephant was his best friend. It was a wild beast, a killer, that set out at a brisk trot in the direction from which the sounds had come.

The sounds that had come to the ears of Tarzan and the ears of Nkima had come also to other ears in the dense forest beyond the gorge. Their owners were slinking through the shaded gloom on silent, stealthy feet to reconnoiter. They came warily, for they knew the sounds meant white men; and many white men with guns were bad medicine. They hoped that there were not too many.

As Tarzan reached the edge of the gorge and looked down upon the scene below, other eyes looked down from the opposite side.

These other eyes saw Tarzan; but the trees and the underbrush hid them from him, and the wind being at his back, their scent was not carried to his nostrils.

Of the two men in the gorge, Marks was the first to see Tarzan. He called Mullargan's attention to him, and the two men watched the ape-man descending slowly toward them. Nkima, sensing trouble, remained at the summit, chattering and scolding. Tarzan approached the two men in silence.

"Wot you want?" demanded Mullargan, reaching for the gun at his hip.

"You kill?" asked Tarzan, pointing at the dead elephant, and in his anger, reverting to the monosyllabic grunts which were reminiscent of his introduction to English many years before.

"Yes—so what?" Mullargan's tone was nasty.

"Tarzan kill," said the ape-man, and stepped closer. He was five feet from Mullargan when the latter whipped his pistol from its holster and fired. But quick as Mullargan had been, Tarzan had been quicker. He struck the weapon up, and the bullet whistled harmlessly into the air; then he tore the gun from the other's hand and hurled it aside.

Mullargan grinned, a twisted, sneering grin. The poor boob was pretty fresh, he thought, getting funny like that with the Heavyweight Champion of the World. "So you're dat Tarzan bum," he said; then he swung that lethal right of his straight for Tarzan's chin.

He was much surprised when he missed. He was more surprised when the ape-man dealt him a terrific blow on the side of the head with his open palm, a blow that felled him, half-stunned.

Marks danced about in consternation and terror. "Get up, you bum," he yelled at Mullargan; "get up and kill him."

Nkima jumped up and down at the edge of the gorge, hurling defiance and insults at the *tarmangani*. Mullargan came slowly to his feet. Instinctively, he had taken a count of nine. Now there was murder in his heart. He rushed Tarzan, and once again the ape-man made him miss; then Mullargan fell into a clinch, pinning Tarzan's right arm and striking terrific blows above one of the ape-man's kidneys, to hurt and weaken him.

With his free hand Tarzan lifted Mullargan from his feet and threw him heavily to the ground, falling on top of him. Steel-thewed fingers sought Mullargan's throat. He struggled to free himself, but he was helpless. A low growl came from the throat of the man upon him. It was the growl of a beast, and it filled the champion with a terror that was new to him.

"Help, Joey! Help!" he cried. "The so-an'-so's killin' me."

Marks was the personification of futility. He could only hop about, screaming: "Get up, you bum; get up and kill him!"

Nkima hopped about too, and screamed; but he hopped and screamed for a very different reason from that which animated Marks, for he saw something that the three men, their whole attention centered on the fight, did not see. He saw a horde of savages coming down out of the forest on the opposite side of the gorge.

The Babangos, realizing that the three men below them were thoroughly engrossed and entirely unaware of their presence, advanced silently, for they wished to take them alive and unharmed. They came swiftly, a hundred sleek warriors, muscled and hard, a hundred splendid refutations of the theory that the eating of human flesh makes men mangy, hairless and toothless.

135

Marks saw them first, and screamed a warning; but it was too late, for they were already upon him. By the weight of their numbers, they overwhelmed the three men, burying Tarzan and Mullargan beneath a dozen sleek dark bodies; but the ape-man rose, shaking them from him for a moment. Mullargan saw him raise a warrior above his head and hurl him into the faces of his fellows, and the champion was awed by this display of physical strength so much greater than his own.

This momentary reversal was brief—there was too many Babangos even for Tarzan. Two of them seized him around the ankles, and three more bore him backward to the ground; but before they succeeded in binding him, he had killed one with his bare hands.

Mullargan was taken with less difficulty; Marks with none. The Babangos bound their hands tightly behind their backs; and prodding them from behind with their spears, drove them up the steep gorge side into the forest.

Little Nkima watched for a moment; then he fled back across the plain.

The gloom of the forest was on them, depressing further the spirits of the two Americans. The myriad close-packed trees, whose interlaced crowns of foliage shut out the sky and the sun, awed them. Trees, trees, trees! Trees of all sizes and heights, some raising their loftiest branches nearly two hundred feet above the carpet of close-packed phyrnia, amoma, and dwarf bush that covered the ground. Loops and festoons of lianas ran from tree to tree, or wound like huge serpents around their boles from base to loftiest pinnacle. From the highest branches others hung almost to the ground, their frayed extremities scarcely moving in the dead air; and other, slenderer cords hung down in tassels with open thread work at their ends, the air roots of the epiphytes.

"Wot you suppose they goin' to do with us?" asked Marks. "Hold us for ransom?"

"Mabbe. I don' know. How'd they collect ransom?"

Marks shook his head. "Then what are they goin' to do with us?"

"Why don't you ask that big bum?" suggested Mullargan, jerking his head in the general direction of Tarzan.

"Bum!" Marks spat the word out disgustedly. "He made a bum outta you, big boy. I wisht I had a bum like that back in Noo York. I'd have a real champeen then. He nearly kayoed you with the flat of his hand. What a haymaker he packs!"

"Just a lucky punch," said Mullargan. "Might happen to anyone."

"He picks you up like you was a flyweight; but when he turns you down you land like a heavyweight, all right. I suppose 'at was just luck."

"He aint human. Did you hear him growl? Just like a lion or somep'n."

"I wisht I knew what they was goin' to do with us," said Marks.

"Well, they aint agoin' to kill us. If they was, they would of done it back there when they got us. There woudn't be no sense in luggin' us somewheres else to kill us."

"I guess you're right, at that."


The footpath that the Babangos followed with their captives wound erratically through the forest. It was scarcely more than eighteen inches wide, a narrow trough worn deep by the feet of countless men and beasts through countless years. It led at last to a rude encampment on the banks of a small stream near its confluence with a larger river. It was the site of an abandoned village in a clearing not yet entirely reclaimed by the jungle.

As the three men were led into the encampment, they were surrounded by yelling women and children. The women spat upon them, and the children threw sticks at them until the warriors drove them off; then, with ropes about their necks, they were tied to a small tree.

Marks, exhausted, threw himself upon the ground; Mullargan sat with his back against the tree; Tarzan remained standing, his eyes examining every detail of his surroundings, his mind centered upon a single subject—escape.

"Cripes," said Marks. "I'm all in."

"You aint never used your dogs enough," said Mullargan,

unsympathetically. "You was always keen on me doin' six miles of road work every day while you loafed in an automobile."

"What was that?" suddenly demanded Marks.

"What's what?"

"Don't you hear it—them groans?" The sound was coming from the direction of the stream, which they could not see because of intervening growth.

"Some guy's got a bellyache," said Mullargan.

"It sounds awful," said Marks. "I wisht I was back in Gawd's country. You sure had a hell of a bright idea—comin' to this Africa. I wisht I knew what they was goin' to do with us."

Mullargan glanced up at Tarzan. "He ain't worryin' none," he said, "and he ought to know what they're goin' to do with us. He's a wild man himself."

They had been speaking in whispers, but Tarzan had heard what they said. "You want to know what they're going to do to you?" he asked.

"We sure do," said Marks.

"They're going to eat you."

Marks sat up suddenly. He felt his throat go dry, and he licked his lips. "Eat us?" he croaked. "You're kiddin', Mister; they aint no cannibals no more, only in movin' pitchers an' story-books."

"No? You hear that moaning coming from the river?"

"Uh-huh."

"That part of it's worse than being eaten."

"They're preparing the meat—making it tender. Those are men or women or little children that you hear—there are several of them. Two or three days ago, perhaps, they broke their arms and legs in three or four places with clubs; then they sank them in the river, tying their heads up to sticks; so they can't drown by accident or commit suicide. They'll leave them there three or four days; then they'll cut them up and cook them."

Mullargan turned a sickly yellowish white. Marks rolled over on his side and was sick. Tarzan looked down on them without pity.

"You are afraid," said Tarzan. "You don't want to suffer.

138

Out on the plain and in the forest are the zebra and elephant that you left to suffer, perhaps for many days."

"But they're only animals," said Mullargan. "We're human bein's."

"You are animals," said the ape-man. "You suffer no more than other animals, when you are hurt. I am glad that the Babangos are going to make you suffer before they eat you. You are worse than the Babangos. You had no reason for hunting the zebra and the elephant. You could not possibly have eaten all that you killed. The Babangos kill only for food, and they kill only as much as they can eat. They are better people than you, who will find pleasure in killing."

For a long time the three were silent, each wrapped in his own thoughts. Above the noises of the encampment rose the moans from the river. Marks commenced to sob. He was breaking. Mullargan was breaking too, but with a different reaction.

He looked up at Tarzan, who still stood, impassive, above them. "I been thinkin', Mister," he said, "about what you was sayin' about us hurtin' the animals an' killin' for pleasure. I aint never thought about it that way before. I wisht I hadn't done it."

A little monkey fled across the hot plain. He made a detour to avoid the lumbering truck following in the wake of the hunters. Shortly thereafter he took to the trees and swung through them close to the edge of the plain. He was a terrified little monkey, constantly on the alert for the many creatures to which monkey meat is an especial delicacy. It was sad that such an ardent nemophilist should be afraid in the forest, but that was because Histah the snake and Sheeta the panther were also arboreal. There were also large monkeys with very bad dispositions, which it were wise to avoid; so little Nkima traveled as quietly and unobtrusively as possible. It was seldom that he traveled, or did anything else, with such singleness of purpose; but today not even the most luscious caterpillar, the most enticing fruits, or even a nest of eggs could tempt him to loiter. Little Nkima was going places, fast. . . .

Melton saw the carcasses of zebra pointing the way the

hunters had gone. He was filled with anger and disgust, and he cursed under his breath. When he came to the edge of the gorge, he saw the wreck of the automobile lying beneath the body of a bull elephant; but he saw no sign of the two men. He got out and went down into the gorge.

Melton was an experienced tracker. He could read a story in a crushed blade of grass or a broken twig. A swift survey of the ground surrounding the wrecked automobile told him a story that filled him with concern—for himself. With his rifle cocked, he climbed back up the side of the gorge toward the truck, turning his eyes often back toward the forest on the opposite side. It was with a sigh of relief that he turned the truck about and started back across the plain.

"The bounders had it coming to them," he thought. "There's nothing I can do about it but report it, and by that time it will be too late."

That night the Babangos feasted, and Tarzan learned from snatches of their conversation that they were planning to commence the preparation of him and the two Americans the following night; but Tarzan was of no mind to have his arms and legs broken. He lay down close to Mullargan.

"Turn on your side," he whispered. "I am going to lie with my back to yours. I'll try to untie the thongs on your wrists; then you can untie mine."

"Oke," said Mullargan.

Out in the forest toward the plain a lion roared, and the instant reaction of the Babangos evidenced their fear of the king of beasts. They replenished their beast-fires and beat their drums to frighten away the marauder. They were not lion men, these hunters of humans; but after a while, hearing no more from the lion, the savages, once again feasting, dancing, drinking, relaxed their surveillance; and Tarzan was able to labor uninterruptedly for hours. It was slow work, for his hands were so bound that he could use the fingers of but one of them at a time; but at least one knot gave to his perserverance. After that it was easier, and in another half-hour Mullargan's hands were free. With two hands, he could work more rapidly; but time was flying. It was long past mid-night. There were signs that the orgy would soon be terminated; then, Tarzan knew, guards would be placed over them. At last he was free. Marks' bonds responded more easily.

"Crawl on your bellies after me," Tarzan whispered. "Make no noise." Mullargan's admission of his regret for the slaughter of the zebra had determined Tarzan to give the two men a chance to escape—that, and the fact that Mullargan had helped to release him. He felt neither liking nor responsibility for them. He did not consider them as fellow-beings, but as creatures further removed from him than the wild beasts with which he had consorted since childhood: those were his kin and his fellows.

Tarzan inched across the clearing toward the forest. Had he been alone, he would have depended upon his speed to reach the sanctuary of the trees where no Babangos could have followed him along the high-flung pathways that the apes of Kerchak had taught him to traverse; but the only chance the two behind him had was that of reaching the forest unobserved.

They had covered scarcely more than a hundred feet when Marks sneezed. Asthmatic, he had reacted to some dust or pollen that their movement had raised from the ground. He sneezed, not once but continuously; and his sneezing was answered by shouts from the encampment.

"Get up and run!" directed Tarzan, leaping to his feet; and the three raced for the forest, followed by a horde of yelling savages.

The Babangos overtook Marks first, the result of neglecting his road-work; but they caught Mullargan too, just before he reached the forest. They caught him because he had hesitated momentarily motivated by what was possibly the first heroic urge of his life, to attempt to rescue Marks. When they were upon him, and both rescue and escape were no longer possible, One-punch Mullargan went berserk.

"Come on, you bums!" he yelled, and planted his famous right on a black chin. Others closed in on him and went down in rapid succession to a series of vicious rights and lefts. "I'll learn you," growled Mullargan, "to monkey with the Heavyweight Champeen of the World!" Then a warrior crept up behind him and struck him a heavy blow across his

141

head with the haft of a spear, and One-punch Mullargan went down and out for the first time in his life.

Tarzan, perched upon the limb of a tree at the edge of the clearing, had been an interested spectator, correctly interpreting Mullargan's act of heroism. It was the second admirable trait that he had seen in either of these *tarmangani,* and it moved him to a more active contemplation of their impending fate. Death meant nothing to him, unless it was the death of a friend, for death is a commonplace of the jungle; and his, the psychology of the wild beast, which, walking always with death, is not greatly impressed by it.

But self-sacrificing heroism is not a common characteristic of wild beasts. It belongs almost exclusively to man, marking the more courageous among them. It was an attribute that Tarzan could understand and admire. It formed a bond between these two most dissimilar men, raising Mullargan in Tarzan's estimation above the position held by the Babangos, whom he looked upon as natural enemies. Formerly, Mullargan had ranked below the Babangos, below Ungo the jackal, below Dango the hyena.

Tarzan still felt no responsibility for these men, whom he had been about to abandon to their fate; but he considered the idea of aiding them, perhaps as much to confound and annoy the Babangos as to succor Mullargan and Marks.

Once again Nkima crossed the plain, this time upon the broad, brown shoulder of Muviro, chief of the white-plumed Waziri. Once again he chattered and scolded, and his heart was as the heart of Numa the lion. From the shoulder of Muviro, as from the shoulder of Tarzan, Nkima could tell the world to go to hell; and did.

From his slow-moving lorry, Melton saw, in the distance, what appeared to be a large party of men approaching. He stopped the lorry and reached for his binoculars.

When he had focused them on the object of his interest, he whistled.

"I hope they're friendly," he thought. One of his boys had told him that the Babangos were raiding somewhere in this territory, and the evidence he had seen around the wrecked automobile seemed to substantiate the rumor. He saw that the boy beside him had his rifle in readiness, and drove on again.

When they were closer, he saw that the party consisted of some hundred white-plumed warriors. They had altered their course so as to intercept him. He thought of speeding up the truck and running through them. The situation looked bad to him, for this was evidently a war party. He called to the boys on top of the load to get out the extra rifles and to commence firing if he gave the word.

"Do not fire at them, Bwana," said one of the boys; "they would kill us all if you did. They are very great warriors."

"Who are they?" asked Melton.

"The Waziris. They will not harm us."

It was Muviro who stepped into the path of the truck and held up his hand.

Melton stopped.

"Where have you come from?" asked the Waziri chief.

Melton told him of the gorge and what he had found in its bottom.

"You saw no other white men than your two friends?" asked Murivo.

"Yesterday, I saw a white man who called himself Tarzan."

"Was he with the others when they were captured?"

"I do not know."

"Follow us," said Muviro, "and camp at the edge of the forest. If your friends are alive, we will bring them back."

Nkima's actions had told Muviro that Tarzan was in trouble, and this new evidence suggested that he might have been killed or captured by the same tribe that had surprised the other men.

Melton watched the Waziri swing away at a rapid trot that would eat up the miles rapidly; then he started his motor and followed. . . .

At the cannibal encampment, the Babangos, sleeping off the effects of their orgy, were not astir until nearly noon. They were in an ugly mood. They had lost one victim, and many of them were nursing sore jaws and broken noses as a result of their encounter with One-punch Mullargan.

The white men were not in much better shape: Mullargan's

143

head ached, while Marks ached all over; and every time he thought of what lay in store for him before they would kill him, he felt faint.

"They breaks our arms and legs in four places," he mumbled, "and' then they soaks us in the drink for three days to make us tender. The dirty bums!"

"Shut up!" snapped Mullargan. "I been tryin' to forget it."

Tarzan, knowing that the Waziri were not far behind him, returned to the edge of the plain to look for them. Alone, and in broad daylight, he knew that not even he could hope to rescue the Americans from the camp of the Babangos. All day he loitered at the edge of the plain; and then, there being no sign of the Waziri, he swung back through the trees toward the cannibal encampment as the brief equatorial twilight ushered in the impenetrable darkness of the forest night.

He approached the camp from a new direction, coming down the little stream in which the remaining victims were still submerged. Above the camp, his nostrils caught the scent of Numa the lion and Sabor the lioness; and presently he made out their dim forms belows him. They were slinking silently toward the scent of human flesh, and they were ravenously hungry. The ape-man knew this, for the scent of an empty lion is quite different from that of one with a full belly. Every wild beast knows this; so it is far from unusual to see lions that have recently fed pass through a herd of grazing herbivores without eliciting more than casual attention.

The silence and hunger of these two stalking lions boded ill for their intended prey.

A dozen warriors approached Mullargan and Marks. They cut their bonds and jerked the two men roughly to their feet; then they dragged them to the center of the camp, where the chief and the witch-doctor sat beneath a large tree. Warriors stood in a semi-circle facing the chief, and behind them were the women and children.

The two Americans were tripped and thrown to the ground upon their backs; and there they were spread-eagled, two warriors pinioning each arm and leg. From the foliage of the tree above, an almost naked white man looked down upon the scene. He was weighing in his mind the chances of effecting a rescue, but he had no intention of sacrificing himself uselessly for these two. Beyond the beast-fires two pairs of yellowish-green unblinking eyes watched. The tips of two sinuous tails weaved to and fro. A pitiful moan came from the stream near by; and the lioness turned her eyes in that direction, but the great black-maned male continued to glare at the throng within the encampment.

The witch-doctor rose and approached the two victims. In one hand he carried a zebra's tail, to which feathers were attached; in the other a heavy club. Marks saw him and commenced to whimper. He struggled and cried out:

"Save me, kid! Save me! Don't let 'em do this to me!"

Mullargan muttered a half-remembered prayer. The witch-doctor began to dance around them, waving the zebra's tail over them and mumbling his ritualistic mumbo-jumbo. Suddenly he leaped in close to Mullargan and swung his heavy club above the pinioned man; then Mullargan, Heavyweight Champion of the World, tore loose from the grasp of the warriors and leaped to his feet. With all the power of his muscles and the weight of his body, he drove such a blow to the chin of the witch-doctor as he had never delivered in any ring; and the witch-doctor went down and out with a broken jaw. A shout of savage rage went up from the assembled warriors, and a moment later Mullargan was submerged by numbers.

The lioness approached the edge of the stream and stretched a taloned paw toward the head of one of the Babangos' pitiful victims, a woman. The poor creature screamed in terror, and the lioness growled horribly and struck. The Babangos, terrified, turned their eyes in the direction of the sounds; and then the lion charged straight for them, his thunderous roar shaking the ground. The savages turned and fled leaving, their two victims and the witch-doctor in the path of the carnivore.

It all happened so quickly that the lion was above Mullargan before he could gain his feet. For a moment the great beast stood glaring down at the prostrate man, who lay paralyzed with fright, staring back into those terrifying eyes. He smelled the fetid breath and saw the yellow fangs and the drooling jowls, and he saw something else—something that filled him with wonder and amazement—as Tarzan launched himself from the tree full upon the back of the great cat.

Mullargan leaped to his feet then and backed away, but was held by fascinated horror as he waited for the lion to kill the man. Marks scrambled up and tried to climb the tree, clawing at the great bole in a frenzy of terror. The lioness had dragged the woman from the stream and was carrying her off into the forest, her agonized screams rising above all other sounds.

Mullargan wished to run away, but he could not. He stood fixed to the ground, watching the incredible. Tarzan's legs were locked around the small of the lion's body, his steel-thewed arms encircling the black-maned neck. The lion reared upon his hind feet, striking futilely at the man-thing upon his back; and mingled with his roaring and his growling were the growls of the man. It was the latter which froze Mullargan's blood.

He saw the lion throw himself to the ground and roll over upon the man in a frantic effort to dislodge him, but when he came to his feet again the man was still there. One-punch Mullargan had witnessed many a battle that had brought howls of approval for the strength or courage of the contestants, but never had he seen such strength and courage as were being displayed by this almost naked man in hand-to-hand battle with a lion.

The endurance of a lion is in no measure proportional to its strength, and presently the great cat commenced to tire. For a moment it stood squarely upon all four feet, panting; and in that first moment of opportunity Tarzan released his hold with one hand and drew his hunting-knife from its scabbard. At the movement, the lion wheeled and sought to seize his antagonist. The knife flashed in the firelight and the long blade sank deep behind the tawny shoulder. Voicing a hideous roar, the beast reared and leaped; and again the blade was driven home. In a paroxysm of pain and rage, the great cat leaped high into the air. Again the blade was buried in its side. Three times the point had reached the lion's heart; and at last it rolled over on its side, quivered convulsively and lay still.

Tarzan sprang erect and placed a foot upon the carcass of his kill, and raising his face to the heavens voiced the hideous victory cry of the bull ape. Marks' knees gave beneath him, and he sat down suddenly. Mullargan felt the hairs on his scalp rise. The Babangos, who had run into the forest to escape the lion, kept on running to escape the nameless horror of the weird cry.

"Come!" commanded Tarzan; and led the two men toward the plain—away from captivity and death and the cannibal Babangos.

Next day, Marks and Mullargan were in camp with Melton. Tarzan and the Waziri were preparing to leave in pursuit of the Babangos, to punish them and drive them from the country.

Before the ape-man left, he confronted the two Americans.

"Get out of Africa," he commanded, "and never come back."

"Never's too damn' soon for me," said Mullargan.

"Listen, Mister," said Marks "I'll guarantee you one hundred G. if you'll come back to Noo York an' fight for me."

Tarzan turned and walked away, joining the Waziri, who were already on the march. Nkima sat upon his shoulder and called the *tarmangani* vile names.

Marks spread his hands, palms up. "Can you beat it, kid?" he demanded. "He turns down one hundred G. cold! But it's a good thing for you he did—he'd have taken that champeenship away from you in one round."

"Who?" demanded One-punch Mullargan. "Dat bum?"

# TARZAN
# AND
# THE JUNGLE MURDERS

*

*

*

*

*

*

## I

### *The Hyena's Voice*

A BRONZED GIANT OF A MAN, naked save for a breech-clout, stalked silently along a forest trail. It was Tarzan, moving through his vast jungle domain in the crisp freshness of the early morning.

The forest was more or less open in this section, with occasional natural clearings in which only a few scattered trees grew. Consequently Tarzan's progress was rapid—rapid, that is, for ground movement.

If the jungle had been thick he would have taken to the trees, and gone hurtling through them with the strength of an ape and the speed of a monkey. For he was Tarzan of the Apes, who, despite his many contacts with civilization since the early days of his young manhood, had retained the fullness of all his jungle ways and powers.

He seemed indifferent to his surroundings, yet this indifference was deceptive, the result of his familiarity with the sights and sounds of the jungle. In reality, every sense in him was on the alert.

Tarzan knew, for example, that a lion was lying in a patch of brush a hundred feet to his left and that the king of beasts lay beside the partially eaten carcass of a slain zebra. He saw neither the lion nor the zebra, but he knew they were there. Usha, the Wind, carried that information to his sensitive nostrils.

Long experience had taught this man of the jungle the characteristic odors of both lion and zebra. The spoor of a lion with a full belly is different from that of a hungry, stalking lion. So Tarzan passed on, unconcerned, knowing that the lion would not attack.

Tarzan preferred the evidence of his nostrils to any other way of finding things out. The eyes of a man could deceive him in the twilight and the night, the ears could be wrongly influenced by imagination. But the sense of smell never failed. It was always right; it always told a man what was what.

It was unfortunate, therefore, that a man could not always be traveling up-wind—either the man himself changed his direction, or the wind itself shifted.

The former case applied to Tarzan now, as he moved across wind to avoid a stream which he was not in the mood to swim. Consequently his preternatural sense of smell, temporarily less useful, yielded place to his other information-bringing senses.

And so, something was borne in upon his hearing that would have escaped all ears but his—the far off cry of Dango, the Hyena.

Tarzan's scalp tingled, as it always did when he heard that unpleasant sound. Toward all other animals, the crocodile alone excepted, Tarzan could have respect—but for Dango, the Hyena, he could have only contempt. He despised the creature's filthy habits and loathed its odor. Chiefly because of this last, he usually avoided the vicinity of Dango whenever he could, lest he be moved to kill a living creature out of pure hate, which he did not consider good cause.

So long as Dango did not commit evil, Tarzan spared him—after all he couldn't kill a beast just because he didn't

149

like that animal's smell, could he? Besides, it was Dango's nature to smell the way he did.

Tarzan was about to change his direction once more, this time to avoid getting close to Dango, when suddenly a new note in Dango's voice caused him to change his mind completely. It was a strange note, it told of something unusual. Tarzan's curiosity was aroused, so he decided to investigate.

He increased his speed. When the forest closed in on him he took to the trees, hurtling through them in great leaps that ate up the distance. The monkeys chattered to him as he went past, and he replied to them with the same rapid sounds, telling them that he had not time to stop. At any other time he might have paused to cavort with the baby monkeys, while the mothers looked on in approval or the fathers tried to inveigle him into playing coconut-catch with them; but now he was in a hurry to find out what had put that strange note into Dango's voice.

Nevertheless, one particularly mischievous simian let fly with a coconut without giving warning. He did not do it viciously, because he knew the quickness of Tarzan's eye. And he was totally unprepared for Tarzan's swift return shot. Tarzan caught the missle and flung it back in almost one and the same motion, and the jungle baseball went through the monkey's grasp to bounce with a hollow thump against the hairy chest.

A chorus of monkey-laughter rose, and the mischievous monkey rubbed his chest ruefully with one hand while he scratched his head sheepishly with the other.

"Play with your brothers," Tarzan sang out. "Tarzan has no time for games today."

And he increased his speed still more. The voices of Dango and his fellows came louder and louder to his ears, their smell grew still more offensive. In mid-air he spat his distaste, but he did not swerve from his course. And at last, at the edge of a clearing, he looked down on a sight that was strange indeed in this African wilderness.

There on the ground lay an aeroplane, partially wrecked. And there, prowling round and round the wreckage, was the source of the smell Tarzan hated—a half dozen slaver-dripping, tongue-lolling hyenas. On soft feet they padded, round and round in restless motion, occasionally jumping high against the plane's side in an obvious effort to get at something within.

Conquering his revulsion, Tarzan dropped lightly to the ground. Soft as the impact was, though, the hyenas heard and turned sharply. They snarled, then retreated a little. It is always the hyena's first impulse to retreat except from things already dead. Then seeing that Tarzan was alone, some of the bolder among them inched forward with bared fangs. There was an old and mutual enmity between this man and the seed of Dango.

Tarzan seemed to pay the hyenas no heed. The bow and quiver of arrows at his back remained unslung. His hunting knife remained in its sheath. He did not even raise his spear in menace. He showed his contempt. But he was watchful. He knew the hyena of old. Cowardly, yes—but when goaded by hunger, capable of sudden daring attack with claw and fang. He smelled their hunger now, and while outwardly he remained contemptuous, inwardly he was vigilant.

Emboldened by Tarzan's outward indifference, the hyenas, moved closer to him. Then, with a sudden rush, the biggest of them leaped for his throat!

Before the wicked fangs could clamp together around his throat, Tarzan shot out a bronzed hand, grabbed the beast's neck. He swung the body once above his head, sent it hurtling with terrific force against the other hyenas, knocking three to the ground. The three were up almost at once but the one remained, and all the hyenas straightway fell upon the broken body of their leader and commenced devouring it. Aye, Tarzan of the Apes knew the best way of handling hyenas.

While they were busy at their loathsome feeding, Tarzan examined the plane and found it was not totally damaged. One wing was crumpled and the landing gear was shattered. But what was true of this thing of wire and metal was not true of the flesh and blood that had guided it—the flesh and blood which the hyenas had been unable to reach. The pilot, encased in his part of the cockpit, still sat at his controls, but his body was bent forward in death, his head resting against the instrument board.

The plane was an Italian army ship. Tarzan made a mental note of the number and insignia. Then clambering onto the wing to reach the cockpit, he drew away the wreckage from the pilot's accidental tomb and examined the man more closely.

"Dead—one, two days," he muttered. "Bullet hole in throat, a little to the left of larynx. Now, that's strange. I'd say this man was wounded while in the air. He lived long enough to land his ship. He had company with him, too. But they didn't shoot him."

It took no special figuring on Tarzan's part to infer that the dead man had not been alone. The ground around the ship showed human footprints, not native ones, either, for the feet had been shod with civilized footgear. Also there were a number of cigarette butts and a piece of a cellophane wrapping.

But the deduction that the pilot had not been shot by his companions required much closer reasoning. On the face of it. it was incredible that it could have happened any other way— if they didn't shoot him, who did? Yet, a shot from his companions would have had to come either from the right side or from the rear. The bullet, however, had penetrated the throat at the left of the larynx.

A low, jungle oath escaped Tarzan.

"Impossible as it may seem," he muttered, "this man was shot while in the air—and not by his companions either. Who did it then?"

Once again he examined the wound. He shook his head, his brow furrowed.

"The bullet came down from above. . . . Now how could that be . . . unless . . . unless it came from another plane. That's it. That must be it! It couldn't have happened in any other way."

A strange mystery, indeed, in the heart of Africa, far from all traveled air-lanes. Tarzan interpreted its sign, as he would have read spoor along jungle trails, and the conclusions he reached were as certain, so certain that he now asked himself:

"Where did the other plane go?"

The sounds the hyenas were making—the tearing of flesh, the snufflings and champings and slaverings, the grinding of their teeth as they devoured one of their own kind—came to Tarzan and he spat his disgust. Almost he was minded to spring out with spear and knife and make an end of them—make food out of the feeders, food for vultures. But he muttered to himself:

"There are things here that are more important. Things that have to do with human beings. They come first."

So he went on with his investigation. He found a single glove, a right-hand glove. He picked it up, opened it, smelled of the inside. His nostrils quivered. Then he dropped the glove—but he would not soon forget what he had learned from it.

He leaped to the ground. Now the sight of the hyenas at their gruesome work was coupled with the sounds they made and augmented by their smell. It was too much for Tarzan. A booming roar broke from his great chest and he hurtled toward the hyenas, spear brandished threateningly. They scattered. He knew they would be back to finish the carcass, but in the meantime, while he finished his survey, he would at least be free of their offensiveness.

Minutely he examined the ground.

"Two men," he said softly. "They started out"—he pointed downward, although he was talking to no one but himself—"from here. And they went"—again he pointed—"this way. The trail is about two days old, but not too cold to follow. I'll follow it."

Several motives animated Tarzan's decision. If still alive, the men who had dropped down from the skies and were now in the jungle, were fellow human beings who might need help. In addition, those men were strangers, and it was Tarzan's business to find out who they were and what they were doing in his domain.

Accordingly he started out with no futher deliberation.

Tantor, the Elephant, trumpeted across his path and stood waiting with ready trunk to swing Tarzan onto his back, but

Tarzan had no time for such luxuries. He could follow the trail better if close to the ground, so he shouted:

"Go back to your herd, Tantor!"

But lest the elephant should feel hurt, Tarzan vaulted upon his back, gave Tantor a quick rub behind the ears, jumped down and was off and away on the trail again. Tantor, content, lumbered off to rejoin his herd, his trunk lifted high.

It was Usha, the Wind, which brought Tarzan his next interruption. Usha, shifting slightly, transmitted to Tarzan's nostrils an altogether new scent—a scent completely at variance with what anyone would have expected in the fastnesses of the African jungle. Straightway Tarzan swerved off the trail to follow up this new sign.

Swiftly the odor grew more pronounced until at last he recognized beyond further doubt the odor of gasoline.

Here again was mystery. Gasoline implied the presence of man, but he detected no man-odor on the breeze. Still, the gasoline scent was a kind of advance-evidence that he had been right in his assumption of the presence of another aeroplane.

The assumption was soon verified by actual sight. There it lay, the mass of crumpled wreckage that had once been a man-made bird, a ship winging through the air above Africa. Now it was broken and twisted—grim evidence of tragedy.

Here, Tarzan knew, was the second half of the puzzle. This was the other plane, which had held the man, who had fired the bullet, which had entered the throat of that other man and killed him. The tail of his plane showed the ravaging effect of machine-gun fire. Yes, quite evidently there had been a fight in the air, an unequal fight, for apparently the man in this second plane had been armed only with a revolver.

Unequal or not however, Man Number Two had managed to escape the fate of Number One. See there, the trampled grass. Number Two had come back to the plane, then gone away.

Tarzan followed the spoor a short way, came to a tangled mass of rope and silk.

"Parachute," he said. "Number Two bailed out."

Tarzan's brain was busy. His eyes held a faraway look as he was reconstructing what must have happened.

"Plane Number One attacked Plane Number Two. That's obvious, since Number One had a machine gun and Number Two did not. Pilot Number Two had a revolver. With it, he shot pilot Number One, who made a forced landing, then died, and was deserted by two companions. The machine-gun bullets forced down Plane Number Two. Its pilot bailed out and landed here, several miles from Number One. All told, then, three men walked away from two planes."

Were they still alive?

"And why has all this happened?" Tarzan wondered. But for that question he could give no answer. He could figure out *what* had happened; but he could not figure out *why*.

And this jungle, he knew, would probably lock the answer away in death. The jungle was harsh to those who did not know her ways. The three men who had been cast away in it had little chance, if they were not dead already.

Tarzan shook his head. He was not satisfied that this should be the answer. Humanitarian impulses stirred his breast. Plane Number Two was English—its pilot was probably English too, just as the other two men were probably Italian. In Tarzan's veins ran English blood.

To Tarzan, the life of a man was no better than the life of an antelope. Tarzan would help an antelope in trouble, and he would help a man in trouble if that man deserved it. The only difference was that an antelope in trouble always deserved help whereas man sometimes did not. But Tarzan could not say one way or another what these men, and in particular the Englishman, deserved.

"Englishman," he said to himself, "you first. Let's hope I can get to you before the lions or the Buiroos do."

So Tarzan set out on the trail of a man whom he did not know. Tarzan set out on the trail of Lieutenant Cecil Giles-Burton.

## II

### The Thread of Fate

Fate is a thread that connects one event with another and one human being with another. The thread that was to lead to Tarzan in the African jungle began in the laboratory of Horace Brown in Chicago. From Tarzan it led back to Lieutenant Burton, from Burton it led back to a man named Zubanev in London, from Zubanev to Joseph Campbell, otherwise known as "Joe the Pooch," from Campbell to Mary Graham who talked too much, and finally from Mary Graham to Horace Brown, whose secretary she was.

It is a long thread, all the way from Chicago to Africa, and there is blood on it and the promise of more blood to come.

Horace Brown was an American inventor. He had a secretary, Mary Graham, who was in his confidence and who talked too much. Horace Brown invented something—something of extreme military importance. Mary knew about it, and Mary went to a party. It was at this party that Mary did her excessive talking.

She meant well, but alas, Mary was not pretty, and usually attempted to make up for this lack of beauty by sparkling conversation. This time, very unfortunately, she sparkled to the wrong man—Joseph Campbell, alias Joe the Pooch.

To Mary a man was a man, and although Campbell was not particularly attractive, his interest flattered her. And she mistook his interest in her conversation for interest in herself.

Horace Brown's invention was an electrical device designed to disrupt the ignition system of any internal combustion engine at any distance up to three thousand feet.

"You can readily see what that would mean in wartime," Mary said brightly, gesturing with her left hand not so much for emphasis as to show that her efficient typist's fingers were naked of either wedding or engagement ring. "No tanks

156

or other motorized equipment of the enemy could approach within a thousand yards. Strafing planes could be brought down before they could inflict any serious damage on airdromes. Bombers, equipped with these machines, would be invulnerable to attack by pursuit planes—"

Mary rambled on, unaware of Lieutenant Cecil Giles-Burton, unaware of Zubanev, unaware of Tarzan of the Apes, unaware of all those people in far off places whose lives she was unconsciously influencing. She was aware only that here was a man who was showing interest in her.

Joseph Campbell, eyes reflecting admiration—admiration for the information he was getting which she mistook for admiration for herself—listened with both ears, a hard head and a flinty heart. He saw possibilities for profit—tremendous possibilities, but he was not yet quite sure how he could go about getting those profits.

"I'd like to see that gadget," he said casually.

"You can't," Mary said. "No one can, at present. It's been dismantled as a precautionary measure against theft. Mr. Brown has retained only the drawings, one set of them."

"Well, I'd like to talk to him anyway," said Campbell, and added with a meaning glance: "It would give us a chance to see more of each other. Perhaps I might even finance Mr. Brown."

Mary shook her head regretfully.

"I'm afraid that's impossible, too. Mr. Brown is on his way to London to negotiate with the British Government. You see, he means for only the two countries to have the invention. . . ."

Thus did Mary Graham innocently weave the first length of fate's bloody thread.

When Joseph Campbell took leave of Mary Graham that night, he promised to call her the following evening. That was the last she heard of him. Joseph Campbell faded out of her life, just as Mary Graham, at this point, fades out of this narrative. . . .

On the other side of the Atlantic a week later, Horace Brown, having arrived at a satisfactory arrangement with the British Government, was assembling his machine in a small machine shop in London. Since it was assumed that no one but himself and the authorities knew what he was doing, no unusual precautions were taken to safeguard him. Two reliable mechanics assisted him during the day. At night he took the plans home with him to the small boarding-house where he had found a room because it was close to his work.

Nikolai Zubanev, a Russian exile, was also a boarder there. He was a mysterious little man, but apparently harmless. Quite evidently the government did not consider him to be harmless, for it was having him watched as a matter of routine, only Zubanev did not know that. Neither did another boarder, a recent arrival from America who had become friendly with Zubanev. Yet, despite the government's watchfulness, Horace Brown one morning was found murdered and his plans missing. Missing, too, were Mr. Zubanev and his new-found acquaintance, Campbell.

The government tapped its many and varied sources of information. A week later Messrs. Campbell and Zubanev were located in Rome, Italy. The meaning of this was plain —they had gone there to sell the stolen plans to the Italian Government. British agents in Rome got busy. Simultaneously, Lieut. Cecil Giles-Burton took off from Croydon in a fast plane for the Italian capital. The newspapers said that he was making a flight to Capetown, Africa.

There was only one man in Italy before whom Campbell and Zubanev wished to lay their proposition, and it wasn't easy to obtain an interview with him. Zubanev, trusting no one, conceived a plan to safeguard the drawings should the Italian authorities decide to take them from him by force. He hid them in the false bottom of a handbag, and left them in his hotel room.

At the interview, the Great Man became intensely interested. A price was agreed upon—such a price as would make both men independent for life, provided, of course, that the experimental machine to be built from the drawings could do what it was designed to accomplish.

Campbell and Zubanev exuded elation as they returned to their apartment.

Their elation, however, died on the threshold as they opened the door to Zubanev's room. Someone had been there during their absence and taken the place apart, forgetting to put it

158

together again. Zubanev rushed to the bag with the false bottom. The bag was there, and so was the false bottom—but the plans were gone!

Frantic, they telephoned the Great Man, and things immediately commenced to happen. Orders were issued to search everyone leaving Rome and to repeat the search at every border. But a certain airport reported than an Englishman, Lieut. Cecil Giles-Burton, had taken off twenty-five minutes before the search order had been received, presumably for Capetown.

A hasty investigation revealed the further fact that the said aviator had been stopping at the same hotel as Campbell and Zubanev, and that he had checked out only about a half hour before their return and discovery of their loss.

Within the hour, Campbell and Zubanev took off in a fast military pursuit plane piloted by a Lieut. Torlini.

# III

### *Broken Wings*

The blue waters of the Mediterranean rolled below Lieut. Cecil Giles-Burton as he winged south toward the African shore. So far, the undertaking had progressed with extraordinary success and it would have been quite simple to circle to the west now, and swing back to London. But there were reasons for his not doing so.

His orders were to continue south to Bangali, where his father was Resident Commissioner. He was to leave the purloined plans with his father and continue on to Capetown, just as if this was really a sporting flight, as the newspapers had announced.

For the British Government thought it unwise to permit a friendly power to suspect that its agents had stolen the plans from under the nose of the Great Man, even though they had originally been stolen from them. And because Lieutenant Burton's father was Resident Commissioner at Bangali, the lieutenant had been selected for the mission. What could be more natural than that the son should stop to visit his father on his flight to Capetown? In fact, the government records would show that he had asked permission to do so.

Although Bangali had an emergency airport, it was off the main traveled air route, and there was a question as to whether or not a plane could be refueled there, so Burton decided to land at Tunis and fill his tanks.

While he was refueling at the Tunis airport, a little crowd of the curious surrounded his ship. The formalities of the French airport were quickly and pleasantly attended to, and while he was chatting with a couple of the officials, a native approached him.

"The Italians," he said in excellent English, "may beat you to Capetown, if you remain here too long."

"Oh," said one of the Frenchmen, "a race. I did not know that."

Burton thought swiftly. He was being pursued! And the Italian Government was seeking to give the impression that it was just a sportsman's race.

"It really isn't an official contest," said Burton, laughing. "Just a private wager with some Italian friends. If I don't want to lose, I'd better be hopping off."

Five minutes later he was in the air again and winging south with wide-open throttle, grateful for the ingenuity and thoughtfulness of his confederates in Rome and the cleverness of their agent, the "native" in Tunis.

Burton had lost half an hour at Tunis, but it would soon be dark, and if his pursuers did not come within sight of him soon, he hoped to lose them during the night. He was flying a straight course for Bangali, which would take him east of an airline course for Capetown and west of the regular airlane from Cairo to the Cape, the route that they might reasonably expect him to fly because of its far greater safety.

Occasionally he glanced back, and finally, in the last rays of the setting sun, he saw the shimmering silver reflected from the lower surface of the wings of an airplane far behind.

All night that plane folowed him, guided by the flames from his exhaust.

It was a faster ship and hung doggedly on his trail.

He wondered what the enemy's plans were. He knew they didn't want him; it was the papers he carried that they wanted. If he could reach Bangali, the plans would be safe, for he would find ample protection there.

But it was not to be. When dawn broke, the pursuing plane had drawn up beside him. Its wing tip almost touched his. He saw that it was an Italian military pursuit plane, piloted by an Italian officer. The two passengers he did not recognize, although he assumed that they were Campbell and Zubanev, whom he had never seen.

Open country lay beneath them, and the Italian officer was motioning him down. He believed that Bangali was not more than fifty miles away. When he shook his head at them, they turned the machine gun on him. He banked and dove, and banked again, coming up under their tail.

His only weapon was a service pistol. He drew it and fired

161

up at the belly of the ship, hoping that he might be lucky enough to sever one of the controls. As the other ship banked and turned, he zoomed up.

They were coming from behind now, and coming fast. He turned and fired four more shots into them, and then a burst of machine-gun fire tore away his rudder and stabilizer. Out of control, his ship went into a spin. He had done his best, but he had failed. Cutting the engine, he bailed out with his parachute and floated gently down to earth.

As he was floating downward, he watched the other ship. It was behaving erratically, and he wondered if he had hit the pilot or damaged the controls. The last he saw of it, it disappeared low over a forest a few miles to the south.

Thus the two ships went down to land at the separate spots where Tarzan of the Apes was afterward to find and wonder over them.

Burton quickly came to his feet and unbuckled the harness of his parachute. He looked about him. No living creature was in sight. He was in the midst of an African wilderness, with only a hazy notion of the distance to Bangali, which lay, he believed, a little east of south.

His plane lay, a crumpled mass of wreckage, a few hundred yards away. He was glad he had cut the engine and that his ship had not burned, for it contained a little food and some extra cartridges. He figured that he was in a hell of a fix, and he was—much worse than he realized.

But the plans for which he had risked his life were buttoned securely inside his shirt. He felt of them to make sure that they were still there. Satisfied, he walked over to the wrecked plane and got ammunition and food.

He set off immediately in the direction in which he thought Bangali lay, for he knew that if his pursuers had made a safe landing they would be looking for him. If Bangali were only fifty miles away, as he hoped, and lay in the direction he believed it did, he felt that he might reasonably expect to reach it on the third day. He prayed that he was not in lion country, and, if there were natives, that they were friendly.

But he was in lion country, and what natives there were were not friendly—and Bangali was three hundred miles away.

# IV

## *Jungle Call*

Two days were to pass before the thread which began with Horace Brown in Chicago, and was already soaked in one spot with Horace Brown's blood, was to reach out and wind itself about the hyena-hating Tarzan in Africa. The third day found Tarzan of the Apes following the cold trail of the Englishman, Cecil Giles-Burton. Then fate played a queer trick.

Cecil Giles-Burton, who had never set foot in Africa before, passed unharmed through the country of the savage Buiroos—but Tarzan of the Apes, born and bred in this land and the master of its lore, was ambushed, wounded and captured!

It happened in this way: Tarzan was approaching a forest growth down-wind, hence the scent-spoor of any life ahead of him could not come to his sensitive nostrils. Thus he could not know that a score of Buiroo warriors were advancing through the forest in his direction. They were hunting, therefore moved silently, so Tarzan neither heard nor smelled them as they came on.

It was at this moment that a lion broke suddenly from the forest a little to his left. Blood was running from a wound in the lion's side, and it was in an ugly mood. The beast bounded past him a few yards, then abruptly turned and charged directly at him.

Tarzan, in perfect calm, raised his short, heavy spear above his right shoulder and waited. And now . . . his back was toward the forest. . . .

It was then that the Buiroos came upon him from behind. . . .

Their surprise was great, but it did not deter their action. Chemungo, son of Mpingu the chief, recognized the

163

white man, recognized him as Tarzan—Tarzan who had once robbed the village of a captive who was to be tortured and sacrificed—Tarzan who had made a fool of Chemungo into the bargain.

Chemungo wasted no time. He hurled his spear, and the white man went down with the weapon quivering in his back. But the other warriors did not forget the lion. With loud shouts they rushed upon him, holding their enormous shields in front of them.

The beast leaped for the foremost warrior, striking the shield and throwing the man to the ground where the shield protected him while his fellows surrounded the lion and drove home their weapons.

Once more the lion charged, and once again a warrior went down beneath his shield, but now a spear found the savage heart and the battle was over.

There was great rejoicing in the village of Mpingu the Chief when the warriors returned with a white prisoner and the carcass of a lion. Their rejoicing, however, was tempered with some misgivings when they discovered that their prisoner was the redoubtable Tarzan.

Some, incited by the village witch doctor, advocated killing the prisoner at once, lest he invoke his powers of magic to do them injury. Others, however, counseled setting him free, arguing that the spirit of the murdered Tarzan might do them infinitely more harm than Tarzan alive.

Torn between two opposing ideas, Mpingu compromised. He ordered the prisoner to be securely bound and guarded, and his wounds treated. If, by the time he got well, nothing untoward had happened, they would treat him as they treated other prisoners; and then there would be dancing— and eating!

Tarzan had stopped bleeding. The wound would have killed an ordinary man, but Tarzan was no ordinary man. Already he was planning his escape.

His bonds were tight, and his captors took great pains to keep them that way. Each night they tightened them anew, wondering at the great strength that enabled the man to loosen them at least enough to cause the blood in his arms and legs to flow less sluggishly.

This nightly tightening of his bonds became a serious problem to Tarzan. It was more than that—it was an insult to his natural dignity.

"A man without the use of his arms," he thought, "is only half a man. A man without the use of his arms and legs is not a man at all. He is a child, who must be fed like a child, as the Buiroos are feeding me."

And Tarzan's heart swelled with the indignity of it, an indignity thrice multiplied at being fed by a degenerate people like the Buiroos. Yet what availed the swelling of Tarzan's heart, if his wrists and ankles could not swell, too—swell and burst his bonds?

Tarzan's great heart burned within his breast, but his brain remained cool.

"They feed me to fatten me," his brain told him. "A man of muscle would make too tough eating for them. So they seek to put over me a layer of succulent fat. Is this a fit end for Tarzan—to wind up in the bellies of Buiroos? No, it is not a fit end for Tarzan—nor will it be the end! Tarzan will surely think of something."

So Tarzan thought of this and that, and dismissed each thought in turn as useless. But his five senses, more highly developed than those of any other men, remained in tune.

Three of those senses did not matter much in his present condition. He could see, but of what use was sight when a man had only the walls of a mean hut to look at? What mattered touch when a man's hands and feet were bound? What good was taste when it meant tasting food not acquired by his own strong hands but fed to him by Buiroos, so that his muscles should take on a layer of fat to melt on their tongues and delight their palates?

No, two senses alone—hearing and smell—still meant something. And over and above them the mysterious sixth sense that Tarzan possessed to a degree unknown to other men.

So the days and nights passed, with Tarzan thinking in his waking hours and thinking even in his dreams. He was more alive than ever to all sounds and all smells; but more important than that, his sixth sense was alive to the jungle and any message it might bring him.

Messages there were many, but he waited for the one that would bring him hope. He heard Sheetah, the Leopard. There was no hope there. He heard Dango again, and smelled the beast with his old disgust. Numa, the Lion, voiced his hunger grunt from far away. Tarzan's keen ears heard it, but the sound was meaningless except to introduce the passing thought that it was nobler to be eaten by a lion than by Buiroos.

Then Tarzan—or rather Tarzan's sixth sense—received another message. A faint glow of surprise appeared in his eyes, his nostrils quivered.

Soon after that, Tarzan began to sway his torso backward and forward, gently, and a low chanting sound began to issue from his lips. The guard at the hut's opening peered in, saw Tarzan's gentle swaying, and asked:

"What are you doing?"

Tarzan interrupted his motion and chant only long enough to say, "Praying." Then he resumed.

The guard reported what he had seen to Mpingu. Mpingu grunted and said that the gods of the Buiroos were more powerful than Tarzan's.

"Let him pray," Mpingu said. "It will not save him. Soon our teeth and tongues will know him."

The guard returned to the hut, resumed his post. Tarzan was still swaying and chanting, only a little louder now. He waited for the guard to tell him not to, but the guard said nothing, wherefore Tarzan knew that his plan was working.

The message still came to him, but now it was more than a message received by his sixth sense. The message was coming to his nostrils now, unmistakable!

But Tarzan was careful. He was sending out a call, but he increased its volume only gradually, so that the illusion of prayer could be kept in the minds of the Buiroos. And so gradually did the sounds he made increase in volume, that from one minute to the next the change was scarcely noticeable.

It was all at once that the Buiroos realized that Tarzan's voice was very loud, and for still another minute they explained it by the supposition that Tarzan could not make his gods listen to him. Then they heard, bursting upon their ear-drums, like thunder when the skies are black and angry, Tarzan's great bellow.

There was sudden quiet. . . .

Deep in the jungle, Tantor, the Elephant, lifted his head to the night breeze, and the forepart of his trunk curled up spasmodically. His ears flapped. He turned partway around to face the breeze fully. Once more he sniffed—and then he trumpeted.

He trumpeted, calling his herd together. They came, stood up-wind with him, listened, heard what he heard. They had wandered far, out of their usual stamping grounds, following their leader submissively, for their leader had been very restless the last few days, as though seeking something, and they had feared to cross his will.

Now they knew what had made him restless and what had drawn him, and now they, too, shook the air with their own trumpetings, trampled the ground with impatience, waiting only the signal from their leader to set out.

Tantor gave the awaited signal—and the herd marched!

It marched quickly, steadily, remorselessly—straight for its goal. It marched without swerving, except for the great trees. The saplings it juggernauted down as if they were match-wood. Straight and true, the great herd marched on the Buiroo village. . . .

Tarzan, in his captive's lair, was the first to hear the thunder of the oncoming herd. His eyes lit up and his lips twisted in a smile. His "prayers" had been heard! His deliverance came on apace—faster, faster—nearer, nearer!

Panicky cries rose in the outer air. Tarzan heard the ripping and rending of wood as the elephants pushed against the village stockade. Crash! A whole section of the stockade came shattering down. The elephants were in!

"Tantor! Tantor!" Tarzan's great voice called. "Tantor! Tantor!" his voice yelled out. "Come to me!"

But Tantor needed no vocal invitation to come to Tarzan. The scent of his man-friend alone was enough, and Tarzan's voice merely confirmed Tantor's knowledge of his presence there. .

Tarzan heard the swoop of Tantor's trunk above him. The entire thatched roof of the hut he was in was swept away. Looking up, Tarzan beheld the tremendous bulk of Tantor, and beyond that the stars of heaven. The next instant Tantor's trunk dipped down, encircled Tarzan, lifted him and hung him up on his back.

Tantor lifted his trunk, waited. Now Tarzan and not Tantor was in command of the herd.

And it was Tarzan, with his great voice, who signaled that it was time to depart. The village was a shambles now, not a hut left standing, and the Buiroos had retreated in terror into the bush. Triumphantly, the herd left the village behind.

Dawn was breaking. Tantor and the herd had done its job. It was the monkeys and not the elephants who loosened Tarzan's bonds, and hopped about him, chattering with delight at seeing him again. Tarzan rubbed Tantor behind the ears, and Tantor knew he was being thanked.

Then, taking leave of his jungle friends, Tarzan swung off into the trees and disappeared from their sight.

There was no use any more, he knew, in following the spoor of the English aviator. Very likely the poor fellow had already died, either of starvation or beneath the fangs and talons of one of the great carnivorous beasts. No, Tarzan's destination now lay elsewhere—specifically in Bangali.

Nights before, while lying captive, he had heard native African drums relaying a message from the Resident Commissioner in Bangali to his friend Tarzan of the Apes—a message for Tarzan to come to Bangali.

# V

## The Safari

How Lieutenant Cecil Giles-Burton survived his aimless wanderings in the jungle was one of those miracles that sometimes happen in Africa. The Dark Continent, cruel to those who did not know her, spared this man. And the section of Fate's thread which bound him indirectly to a talkative maiden in far-off Chicago was not yet moistened with his own blood.

On two occasions Burton met lions. In each case, fortunately, a tree was handy, and he climbed it. One of those lions had been ravenously hungry and was on the hunt. Burton was treed by it for a whole day. He thought he would die of thirst.

But at last the lion's patience was snapped by its own hunger, and it went off after less difficult game.

The other lion Burton need not have worried about. Its belly was full and it would have paid no attention even to a fat zebra, its favorite food. But Burton, unlike Tarzan, could not tell the difference between a hungry lion and a sated one. Also, like most people ignorant of jungle ways, he held the notion that all lions were man-eaters and went about killing every living creature they could reach.

The getting of food was Burton's chief problem. He lost weight rapidly. He ate many strange things, such as locusts, and came to understand that a hungry man will eat anything.

The days passed swiftly, and he was still searching for Bangali; but he was searching in the wrong direction.

His clothes hung in rags. His hair and beard grew long. But his courage remained. Thin as a rail, he was still full of hope as one morning he sat upon a hillside looking down into a little valley.

His hearing had sharpened since his sojourn in the

jungle, and now, suddenly, he heard sounds coming from the upper end of the valley. He looked—and saw men.

Men! Human beings! The first he had seen in days and days! His heart pounded, swelled in his now bony chest. His first impulse was to jump up and run down to them, crying aloud his joy. Then he restrained himself. Africa had taught him caution. Instead of rushing down, he concealed himself behind a bush and watched. He would look before he leaped.

It was a long file of men. As they came closer, he saw that some of them wore sun-helmets. But the majority of them wore not much of anything. He noted that those who wore the least clothing carried the heaviest burdens.

He knew what he was seeing now. It was a safari—a safari of white men and blacks.

Now he no longer hesitated. He rushed down to meet it.

The column was headed by a native guide and a group of whites. There were two women among the whites. Behind them trooped the long file of porters and *askaris*.

"Hello! Hello!" Burton shouted in a cracked voice. Tears came to his eyes and he choked, stumbling toward them with arms outstretched.

The safari halted and awaited his coming. No answering shouts of greeting came to him. He slowed his pace. Something of his habitual English reserve returned to him. He wondered at their lack of enthusiasm.

"How awful," one of the women—no more than a girl—exclaimed at the soiled sight of him. But the exclamation was less in pity than in impolite shock at his scarecrow appearance.

Lieutenant Burton stiffened and his cracked lips twisted in a crooked smile that held a little bitterness. Was this the way a castaway was received by his own kind? Lieutenant Burton, looking at the girl, said quietly:

"I am sorry, Lady Barbara, that in your shock at my dirty rags, you fail to see that a human being is wearing them."

The girl stared at him, aghast. Over her face spread a flush.

"You know me?" she said unbelievingly.

"Quite well. You are Lady Barbara Ramsgate. That gentleman—or am I wrong in using the word?—is your brother, Lord John. The others I do not know."

"He must have heard rumors about our safari," one of the other men interposed. "That's how he knows the names. Well, man, what's your story? I suppose your safari deserted you, and you're lost and hungry, and want to join up with our safari. You're not the first derelict we picked up—"

"Stop it, Gault," John Ramsgate snapped in an angry voice. "Let the man tell his story."

Lieutenant Burton shook his head. He sent a burning glance at each of them in turn.

"As snobbish in Africa as in London," he said softly. "One of your porters, meeting me like this, would not have asked questions, would have given me food and water even if it meant going without it himself."

Gault opened his mouth to make a hot retort, but the girl stopped him. She looked ashamed.

"I'm sorry," she said. "We've all been under a strain and I'm afraid our veneer has cracked a bit to reveal that we're not as nice as we think we are underneath. I'll order food and water for you immediately."

"No hurry now," Burton said. "I'll answer your unspoken questions first. I was flying from London to Capetown, and was forced down. I have been wandering around ever since, trying to find Bangali. You are the first human beings I've seen. Permit me to introduce myself. My name is Burton— Lieutenant Cecil Giles-Burton, of the Royal Air Force."

"Impossible!" Lady Barbara exclaimed. "You can't be."

"We know Burton," said Lord John. "You don't look anything like him."

"Blame Africa for that. I think if you look closely enough, you'll recognize your week-end guest at Ramsgate Castle."

And Lord John, looking closer, finally murmured, "Gad, yes," and stretched out his hand. "My apologies, old fellow."

Burton did not take the hand. His shoulders sagged. He was ashamed of these people.

"That hand which you now offer to Lieutenant Burton should have been offered to the derelict stranger," he said quietly. "I'm afraid I can't shake it sincerely."

"He's right," Lord John said to his sister, and she nodded meekly. "We're terribly sorry, Burton. I'd be honored very much if you took my hand, Lieutenant."

So Burton shook his hand, and they all felt better. Lady Barbara introduced him to the man who stood at her side— Duncan Trent.

After eating, Burton met the other members of the safari. There was a tall, broad-shouldered man who was called Mr. Romanoff, and it was Romanoff who gave Burton the astounding information that Bangali was fully two hundred miles away. Romanoff imparted this information while being shaved by his valet, Pierre. Evidently this Russian expatriate traveled in style.

Burton learned further that this safari was really two safaris.

"We ran into the Romanoff safari two weeks ago, and since we were both headed in the same direction, for Bangali, we joined forces. The difference is that the Romanoff safari hunts with guns while we hunt only with cameras."

"Silly idea," said Trent, who was evidently interested in Lady Barbara emotionally. "John could have gone to the zoo and taken his silly pictures without all this walking and insect bites."

Burton further learned that Gerald Gault, the man who had spoken so sneeringly to him at first, was Romanoff's guide. There was another Russian in the safari, Sergei Godensky, a professional photographer.

The interest of Burton was drawn to two other white men. These were the other derelicts that had been mentioned. Their names were Smith and Peterson. They had told a story of their native boys deserting them.

"They don't look very gay," Burton said.

"They don't like to do their share of the work, either," John Ramsgate snapped. "Burton, you won't blame us so much for our conduct when you learn more about this rather mixed safari. Romanoff's man, Gault, is domineering and sarcastic. Everybody hates him. Pierre and my valet, Tomlin, are both in love with Violet, Barbara's maid. And I think there's no love lost between Godensky and Romanoff. All told, I wouldn't call it a very happy family."

Coffee and cigarettes followed the dinner. Burton stretched and inhaled deeply.

"To think," he said, "that only this morning I was expecting to starve to death. One never knows what Fate has in store for one."

Unconsciously he patted his shirt over his heart, where the plans for Horace Brown's invention reposed.

"Perhaps it's just as well that we can't look into the future," said Lady Barbara.

It was just as well, so far as Burton's peace of mind was concerned.

Days passed. Burton grew very fond of John Ramsgate and especially fond of Barbara. Duncan Trent began to wear a scowl. In Burton he detected a rival.

Then trouble broke out in the safari over the maid, Violet, when Godensky made advances to her which she made clear she did not want. Burton, accidentally coming upon them, knocked Godensky down. Godensky, in a raging fury, drew his knife. Then Lady Barbara came suddenly upon the scene. Godensky put back his knife and walked away sullenly.

"You've made an enemy," cautioned Barbara.

Burton shrugged his shoulders. He had been through so much already that one more enemy didn't matter.

But he had made more than one enemy. Trent came to him and told him in no uncertain terms to keep away from Lady Barbara.

"I think we can leave it to Lady Barbara to select what company she wants to keep," Burton said quietly.

Tomlin, attracted by the conversation, came out of his tent. He saw Trent strike at Burton, saw Burton smash Trent down.

"Get into your tent and cool off," Burton snapped to Trent, and entered his own tent.

The next morning, Ramsgate notified Godensky that he would not need his services after they reached Bangali. Everyone else ignored Godensky, even the two derelicts, Smith and Peterson, and he marched alone all day, nursing his anger. Duncan Trent brought up the rear of the column, glum and brooding.

173

Everyone seemed out of sorts, and the long trek under the hot, merciless sun did nothing to soothe jangled nerves. The carriers lagged, and Gault spent most of his time running up and down the line cursing and abusing them. Finally he lost his temper and knocked one of them down. When the man got up, Gault knocked him down again. Burton, who was nearby, interfered.

"Cut it out," he ordered.

"You mind your own damned business. I'm running this safari," retorted Gault.

"I don't care whose safari you're running. You're not going to abuse the men."

Gault swung. Burton blocked the blow, and the next instant Gault was sent sprawling with a smashing left to the jaw. It was Burton's third fight since he had joined the safari. Three knockdowns—three enemies.

"I'm sorry, Ramsgate," Burton said, later. "I seem to be getting into trouble with everyone."

"You did just right," said Ramsgate approvingly.

"I'm afraid you've made a real enemy there, Cecil," said Lady Barbara. "I understand Gault has a pretty bad reputation."

"One enemy more makes no difference any longer. We'll be in Bangali tomorrow."

They talked for a few minutes longer and then bidding each other good night, went to their tents. Burton was happy. He knew that he had never been so happy before in his life. Tomorrow he would see his father. Tomorrow he would fulfill his mission; and he was in love. A serene quiet lay upon the camp, over which a drowsy *askari* kept watch. From far away came the roar of a hunting lion, and the man threw more wood upon the fire.

# VI

## *The Coming of Tarzan*

It was just before dawn, and it was very cold. The *askari* on guard was even more sleepy than the man he had relieved. Because it was cold, he sat very near the fire with his back against a log, and sitting there, he fell asleep.

When he awoke, he was so astounded and startled by the sight that met his eyes that he was for the moment incapable of any action. He just sat there, wide-eyed, looking at an almost-naked white man who squatted near him, warming his hands at the fire. Where had this aparition come from? It had not been there a moment before. The *askari* thought that perhaps he was dreaming. But, no. The visitor was too real, of such an immense physique.

The lips of the stranger parted.

"Whose safari is this?" he asked in the Swahili dialect.

The *askari* found his voice.

"Who are you? Where did you come from?" Suddenly his eyes went even wider and his jaw dropped. "If you are a demon," he said, "I will bring you food, if you will not harm me."

"I am Tarzan," said the stranger. "Whose safari is this?"

"There are two," replied the *askari*, his eyes filled with awe. "One is the safari of *Bwana* Romanoff, and the other is the safari of *Bwana* Ramsgate."

"They are going to Bangali?" asked Tarzan.

"Yes. Tomorrow we shall be in Bangali."

"They are hunting?"

"*Bwana* Romanoff hunts. *Bwana* Ramsgate takes pictures."

Tarzan looked at him for a long time before he spoke again, and then he said:

"You should be whipped for falling asleep while on guard."

"But I was not asleep, Tarzan," said the *askari*. "I only closed my eyes because the light of the fire hurt them."

"The fire was nearly out when I came," said Tarzan. "I put more wood upon it. I have been here a long time and you were asleep. *Simba* could have come into camp and carried someone away. He is out there now, watching you."

The *askari* leaped to his feet and cocked his rifle.

"Where? Where is *Simba?*" he demanded.

"Can't you see his eyes blazing out there?"

"Yes, Tarzan, I see them now." He raised his rifle to his shoulder.

"Do not shoot. You might accidentally hit him only to wound him, and then he would charge. Wait."

Tarzan picked up a stick, one end of which was blazing, and hurled it out into the darkness. The eyes disappeared.

"If he comes back, shoot over his head. That may frighten him away."

The *askari* became very alert, but he was watching the stranger quite as much as he was watching for the lion. Tarzan warmed himself by the fire.

After awhile the wind freshened and swung into a new quarter. Tarzan raised his head and sniffed the air.

"Who is the dead man?" he asked.

The *askari* looked around him quickly, but saw no one. His voice trembled a little as he answered.

"There is no dead man, *Bwana*," the *askari* protested.

"There is a dead man over there in that part of camp," said Tarzan, nodding toward the tents of the whites.

"There is no dead man, and I wish that you would go away with your talk of death."

The other did not answer. He just squatted there, warming his hands.

"I must go and awaken the cooks," the *askari* said, presently. "It is time."

Tarzan said nothing, and the *askari* went to awaken the cooks. He told them there was a demon in the camp, and when they looked and saw the white man squatting there by the fire, they, too became intensely frightened. They were still more frightened when the *askari* told them that the demon had said there was a dead man in the camp. They woke up all the other boys, for in numbers there is a greater sense of security.

Ramsgate's headman went to his master's tent and awakened him.

"There is a demon in camp, *Bwana*," he said, "and he says there is a dead man here. There is no dead man in camp, is there, *Bwana*?"

"Of course not—and there are no demons either. I'll be out in a moment."

Ramsgate dressed hurriedly and came out a few moments later to see the men huddled together fearfully, looking toward the fire, where the almost naked gigantic white man squatted. Ramsgate walked toward him, and as he approached the other arose, courteously.

"May I inquire," said Ramsgate, "who you are and to what we owe the pleasure of this visit?" Ramsgate had learned a lesson from Burton on how to treat strangers.

The other motioned toward the fire.

"That is the reason for my visit," he said. "It is unusually cold in the forest tonight."

"Who are you, anyway, man, and what are you doing running around naked in the forest at night?"

"I am Tarzan," replied the stranger. "What is your name?"

"Ramsgate. What is the story you have been telling our boys about there being a dead man in the camp?"

"It is true. There is a dead man in one of those tents. He has not been dead very long."

"But how do you know that? What gives you that queer idea?"

"I can smell him," said Tarzan.

Ramsgate shivered, looked around the camp. The boys were still huddled together at a little distance, watching them; but otherwise everything appeared in order.

He looked again at the stranger, a little more closely this time, and saw that he was fine-looking and intelligent-appearing. Yet he was certain that the man was crazy, probably one of those human derelicts who are found occasionally even in civilized surroundings, wandering naked in the woods.

177

They are usually called wildmen, but most of them are only harmless halfwits. However, Ramsgate thought, remembering Burton's lesson, the best thing to do would be to humor this man and give him food.

He turned and called to the boys.

"Hurry up with that chuck. We want to get an early start today."

Several of the whites had been aroused by the noise in the camp and were straggling from their tents. Gault was among them. He came over toward the fire, followed by the others.

"What have we here, m'Lord?"

"This poor devil got cold and came in to the fire," said Ramsgate. "It's perfectly all right, he's welcome. Will you see that he gets breakfast, Gault?"

"Yes, sir." Gault's meekness surprised Ramsgate.

"And say, Gault, will you have the boys awaken the others? I'd like to get an early start this morning."

Gault turned toward the boys and called out some instructions in Swahili. Several of the boys detached themselves and went to the tents of their masters to awaken them. Tarzan had resumed his place by the fire, and Ramsgate had gone to talk with the *askari* who had been on guard.

He had just started to question the man, when he was interrupted by a shout from the direction of the tents of the whites and saw Burton's boy running excitedly toward him.

"Come quick, *Bwana*," shouted the boy. "Come quick!"

"What is it? What's the matter?" demanded Ramsgate.

"I go in tent. I find *Bwana* Burton lie on floor, dead!"

Ramsgate dashed for Burton's tent, with Tarzan close at his elbow. Gault was directly behind them.

Burton's body, clad only in pajamas, lay face down upon the floor. A chair had been upset and there were other evidences of a fierce struggle.

While the three men were busily examining the body, Romanoff and Trent entered the tent.

"This is terrible," Romanoff exclaimed, shuddering. "Who could have done it?"

178

Trent said nothing. He just stood there, staring down at the body.

Burton had been stabbed in the back, the knife entering under the left shoulder blade from below and piercing the heart. There were black and blue marks on his throat, showing that the murderer had choked him to prevent him from making any outcry.

"Whoever did this must have been a very strong man," said Romanoff. "Lieutenant Burton was himself very powerful."

Amazed, then, they saw the white stranger take command of the situation.

Tarzan lifted the body to the cot and covered it with a blanket. Then he bent low and examined the marks on Burton's throat. He went out and they followed him, mystified and frightened.

As they left the tent, before which practically the entire safari had congregated, Ramsgate saw his sister coming toward them from her tent.

"What's the matter?" she asked, "What has happened?"

Ramsgate stepped to her side. "Something pretty terrible has happened, Babs," he said, avoiding her questioning glance. Then he led her back to her tent and told her.

Gault gruffly ordered the men back to their duties, summoned all the *askaris* who had been on guard during the night and questioned them. The other whites were gathered around them, but only Tarzan understood the questions and the answers, which were in Swahili.

There had been four *askaris* on duty during the night, and all insisted that they had seen or heard nothing unusual, with the exception of the last one, who reported that the strange white man had entered the camp just before dawn to warm himself at the fire.

"Did you see him all the time he was in camp?" demanded Gault.

The man hesitated.

"The fire hurt my eyes, *Bwana*, and I closed them. But only for a moment. All the rest of the time I saw him squatting by the fire, warming himself."

"You are lying," said Gault. "You were asleep."

"Perhaps I slept a little, *Bwana*."

"Then this man might have had time to go to the tent and murder *Bwana* Burton?"

Gault spoke plainly because he did not know that Tarzan understood Swahili.

"Yes, *Bwana*," replied the black. "He might have. I do not know. But he knew there was a dead man there before anyone else knew it."

"How do you know that?"

"He told me so, *Bwana*."

"The man was dead before I came into camp," said Tarzan calmly.

Gault was startled.

"You understand Swahili?" he asked.

"Yes."

"Nobody knows how long you were in camp. You—"

"What's all this about?" interrupted Romanoff. "I can't understand a word. Wait, here comes Lord John. He should carry on this investigation. Lieutenant Burton was his countryman."

Ramsgate and Romanoff listened intently while Gault repeated what the *askari* had told him. Tarzan stood leaning upon his spear, his face impassive. When Gault had finished, Ramsgate shook his head.

"I see no reason to suspect this man," he said. "What motive could he have had? It certainly wasn't robbery, for Burton had nothing of value. And it couldn't have been revenge, for they didn't even know each other."

"Perhaps he's batty," suggested Smith. "Nobody but a nut would run around naked in the woods. And you can't never tell what nuts will do."

Trent nodded. "Dementia praecox," he said, "with homicidal mania."

Lady Barbara, dry-eyed and composed, came and stood beside her brother. Violet was with her, red-eyed and sniffling.

"Have you learned anything new?" Lady Barbara asked her brother.

Ramsgate shook his head.

"Gault thinks this man might have done it."

Lady Barbara looked up. "Who is he?" she asked.

"He says his name is Tarzan. He came into camp some time during the night. Nobody seems to know when. But I don't see any reason to suspect him. He could not possibly have had any motive."

"There are several here who might have had a motive," said Lady Barbara bitterly. She looked straight at Trent.

"Barbara!" Trent exclaimed. "You don't think for a moment that I did this?"

"He was ready to kill him once, m'Lord," said Tomlin to Ramsgate. "I was there, sir. I saw Burton knock him down. They were quarreling about her Ladyship."

Trent looked uncomfortable. "It's preposterous," he protested. "I'll admit I lost my temper, but after I cooled off I was sorry."

Violet pointed an accusing finger at Godensky.

"He tried to kill him, too! He said he'd kill him. I heard him."

"As far as that goes, Gault, here, threatened to get him, too," said Romanoff. "They didn't all kill him. I think the thing for us to do is present ourselves to the authorities at Bangali, and let them thrash the matter out."

"That's all right with me," said Gault. "I didn't kill him, and I don't know that this fellow did. But it's certainly mighty funny that he was the only one in camp to know that Lieutenant Burton was dead."

"There was another who knew," said Tarzan.

"Who was that?" demanded Gault.

"The man who killed him."

"I'd still like to know how you knew he was dead," said Gault.

"So shoult I," said Ramsgate. "I must say that that looks a little suspicious."

"It's quite simple," said Tarzan, "but I'm afraid none of you would understand. I am Tarzan of the Apes. I have lived here nearly all my life under precisely the same conditions as the other animals. Animals are dependent upon certain senses much more than are civilized man. The hearing of some of them is exceptionally keen. The eyesight of others is remarkable. But the best developed of all is the sense of smell.

"Without at least one of these senses highly developed, one couldn't survive for long. Man, being naturally among the most helpless of animals, I was compelled to develop them all. Death has its own peculiar odor. It is noticeable almost immediately after life has ceased. While I was warming myself at the fire and talking to the *askari*, the wind freshened and changed. It brought to my nostrils the evidence that a dead man lay a short distance away, probably in one of the tents."

"Nuts," said Smith disgustedly.

Godensky laughed nervously.

"He must think we're crazy, too, to believe a story like that."

"I think we've got our man all right," said Trent. "A maniac doesn't have to have a motive for killing."

"Mr. Trent's right," agreed Gault. "We'd better tie him up and take him along to Bangali with us."

None of these men knew Tarzan. None of them could interpret the strange look that came suddenly into his gray eyes. As Gault moved toward him, Tarzan backed away. Then Trent drew his pistol and covered him.

"Make a false move and I'll kill you," Trent said.

Trent's intentions may have been of the best, but his technique was faulty. He was guilty, among others, of two cardinal errors. He was too close to Tarzan, and he did not shoot the instant that he drew his gun.

Tarzan's hand shot out and seized his wrist. Trent pulled the trigger, but the bullet plowed harmlessly into the ground. Then he cried out in anguish and dropped the weapon when the ape-man applied more pressure. It was all done very quickly, and then Tarzan was backing away from them holding Trent as a shield in front of him.

They dared not shoot for fear of hitting Trent. Gault and Ramsgate started forward. Tarzan, holding the man with one hand, drew his hunting knife.

"Stay where you are," he said, "or I kill."

His tone was quiet and level, but it had the cutting edge of a keen knife. The two men stopped, and then Tarzan backed away toward the forest that came down to the edge of the camp.

"Aren't you going to do something?" shouted Trent. "Are you going to let this maniac carry me off into the woods and butcher me?"

"What shall we do?" cried Romanoff to no one in particular.

"We can't do anything," said Ramsgate. "If we go after him, he'll surely kill Trent. If we don't, he may let him go."

"I think we ought to go after them," said Gault, but no one volunteered, and a moment later Tarzan disappeared into the forest dragging Trent with him. . . .

The safari did not get an early start that morning, and long before they got under way Trent came out of the forest and rejoined them. He was still trembling from fear.

"Give me a spot of brandy, John," he said to Ramsgate. "I think that demon broke my wrist. God, I'm about done up. That fellow's not human. He handled me as though I were a baby. When he was sure no one was following us, he let me go. And then he took to the trees just like a monkey. I tell you, it's uncanny."

"Did he harm you in any way after he took you out of camp?" Ramsgate wanted to know.

"No. He just dragged me along. He never spoke once, never said a word. It was like—why, it was like being dragged off by a lion."

"I hope we've seen the last of him," said Ramsgate hopefully.

"Well, there's not much doubt about that," replied Trent. "He killed poor Burton, all right, and he's made a clean getaway."

The safari moved slowly, four carriers bearing the body of Burton on an improvised stretcher. It brought up the rear of the column, and Barbara walked ahead with her brother so she would not have to see it.

They did not reach Bangali that day, and had to make another camp. Everyone was depressed. There was no laughing or singing among the native boys, and very shortly after the evening meal everyone turned in for the night.

About midnight the camp was aroused by wild shouting and a shot. Then Smith came running from the tent he shared with Peterson. Ramsgate leaped from his cot and ran out into the open in his pajamas, almost colliding with Smith.

"What's the matter, man? For God's sake, what's happened?"

"That crazy giant," cried Smith. "He was here again. He killed poor Peterson this time. I shot at him. I think I hit him, but I don't know. I couldn't be sure."

"Where did he go?" snapped Ramsgate.

"Off there, into the jungle," panted Smith, pointing.

Ramsgate shook his head.

"There's no use following," he said. "We could never find him."

They went into Peterson's tent and found him lying on his cot, stabbed through the heart while he slept. There was no more sleep in camp that night and the whites as well as the *askaris* stood guard.

# VII

### Murder Will Out

In Bangali, Tarzan sat in the bungalow of Col. Gerald Giles-Burton.

"The shock of your news was not as great as it might have been," said Colonel Burton. "I'd given my boy up for dead a long while ago. Yet, to know that he was alive all the time, and almost here—that's what is hard to bear. Did they have any idea who killed him?"

"They're all pretty sure I did it."

"Nonsense," said Burton.

"There are three men in the safari he had trouble with. They all threatened to get him. But from what I heard, the threats were all made in the heat of anger, and probably didn't mean anything. Only one of them might have thought he had reason to kill."

"Who was that?" asked Burton.

"A chap by the name of Trent, who was in love with Lady Barbara. That was the only real motive, so far as I could learn."

"Sometimes a very strong motive," said Burton.

"However," continued Tarzan, "Trent didn't kill your son. He couldn't have. If the murderer was in camp, I could have found him if they hadn't run me out."

"Will you remain here and help me find him when the safari gets in?"

"Of course. You didn't need to ask."

"There is something else I think you ought to know. At the time that he was lost, my son was carrying some very important papers for the Government. He was ostensibly flying from London to Capetown, but his instructions were to stop here and leave the papers with me."

185

"And he was being pursued by three men in an Italian military plane," said Tarzan.

"Gad, man! How did you know that?" demanded Burton.

"I ran across both planes. Your son's plane was shot down, but he had bailed out safely. I found his parachute near the plane. But before he bailed out, he shot the pilot of the other plane. The fellow brought his plane down safely before he died. I found him still sitting at the controls. The two men with him got out all right. One of them may have been hurt a little, for I noticed that he limped, but he might have been lame before. That, of course, I do not know."

"Did you see them?" asked Burton.

"No. I followed their tracks for a little way until I came across your son's ship. Then, knowing he was an Englishman, or believing so because he was piloting an English plane, I started off after him. You see, he had landed in lion country. You know, the Buiroo country."

"Yes; and the Buiroos are worse than the lions."

"Yes," said Tarzan, reminiscing, "I've had business with them before. They nearly put an end to me this time. After I got away from them I started for Bangali again, and early this morning I stumbled onto this safari."

"Do you think those two men had a chance to get the papers away from my son?"

"No. They were following different trails. They are probably both dead by this time. It's bad country where they came down. They were a couple of Italians, I suppose."

Colonel Burton shook his head.

"No. One was an American and the other was a Russian. Their names were Campbell and Zubanev. I got a full report on them from London. They were wanted for espionage and murder back there."

"Well, I don't think they'll bother anyone again," said Tarzan. "And in the morning you'll have the papers."

"Yes, I'll have the papers," said Burton sadly. "It is strange, Tarzan, how little we appreciate happiness until we lose it. I'm not vindictive, but I'd like to know who killed my son."

"Africa is a large place, Burton," said the ape-man, "but

if the man who murdered your boy is still alive, I'll get him before he gets out of Africa. I promise you that."

"If you can't find him, no one can," said Burton. "Thanks, Tarzan."

Tarzan shook Burton's hand warmly.

Eight stretcher bearers, carrying the bodies of Cecil Burton and Peterson brought up the rear of the safari as it halted just on the outskirts of Bangali and prepared to go into camp.

Ramsgate and Romanoff went immediately to report to Colonel Burton. They found him sitting in his office, a screened veranda along one side of his bungalow. He stood up as they entered and held out his hand to the young Englishman.

"Lord John Ramsgate, I presume," he said, then turning to the Russian, "and Mr. Romanoff. I have been expecting you gentlemen."

"We come on a very sad mission, Colonel Burton," said Ramsgate, a catch in his voice.

"Yes, I know," said Burton.

Ramsgate and Romanoff looked astonished.

"You know!" exclaimed Romanoff.

"Yes. Word was brought to me last night."

"But that is impossible," said Ramsgate. "We must be referring to different things."

"No. We are both referring to the murder of my son."

"Extraordinary!" exclaimed Ramsgate. "I don't understand. But Colonel, we are pretty sure now that we know who the murderer is. Last night there was another similar murder committed in our camp, and one of the members of our safari saw the murderer in the act of committing the crime. He fired at him, and thinks that he hit him."

At this moment the door of the bungalow opened and Tarzan stepped suddenly out onto the veranda!

Ramsgate and Romanoff both leaped to their feet.

"There's the man! There's the murderer!" cried Ramsgate. Colonel Burton shook his head.

"No, gentlemen," he said quietly. "Tarzan of the Apes would not have murdered my son, and he could not have

187

murdered the other man because he was here in my bungalow all last night!"

"But," said Romanoff, "Smith said that he saw this man and recognized him when Peterson was murdered last night."

"Well, in a moment of excitement like that," said Burton, "and in the darkness, a man might easily make a mistake. Suppose we go to your camp and question some of the people involved. I understand that three of them had either attacked or threatened my son."

"Yes," said Ramsgate. "Both my sister and I wish a most thorough investigation be made, and I am sure that Mr. Romanoff feels as we do about it."

Romanoff inclined his head in assent.

"You will come with us, of course, Tarzan?" asked Burton.

"If you wish," Tarzan replied.

It was with mixed emotions that the members of the safari saw Tarzan enter the camp with Ramsgate, Romanoff and Colonel Burton, and a detail of native constabulary.

"They got him," said Gault to Trent. "That was quick work."

"They ought to handcuff him," said Trent, "or he'll get away just as he did before. They haven't even taken his weapons away from him."

At Colonel Burton's suggestion all the whites in the party were gathered together for questioning. While they were being summoned Tarzan carefully examined the body of Peterson. He looked particularly at the man's hands and feet. Then he scrutinized the wound over the heart. Just for a moment he bent low over the body, his face close to the sleeve of the man's tunic. Then he returned to where the company was gathered in front of Colonel Burton.

One by one, the English official questioned them. He listened intently to the evidence of Violet, Tomlin and Lady Barbara. He questioned Godensky, Gault and Trent. He questioned Smith about the murderer of Peterson.

"I understand that you said you saw this man kill Peterson." He indicated Tarzan.

"I thought it was him," said Smith, "but I might have been mistaken. It was very dark."

"Well, now, as to my son," said Burton. "Is there anyone here who cares to make a direct charge of murder against any individual?"

Lady Barbara Ramsgate stiffened.

"Yes, Colonel," she said. "I charge Duncan Trent with the murder of Cecil Giles-Burton."

Trent paled considerably, but did not speak. All eyes were turned upon him. Tarzan bent close and whispered something in Burton's ear. The latter nodded.

"Tarzan wishes to ask a few questions," said Burton. "You will please answer them as you would if I asked them."

"May I see your knife?" asked Tarzan, pointing at Pierre.

"I do not carry one, sir."

"And yours?" He indicated Gault.

Gault withdrew his knife from its scabbard and handed it to the ape-man, who examined it for a moment and then returned it. Then he asked for Tomlin's knife; but Tomlin did not carry one. In rapid succession he asked for and examined the knives of Smith, Godensky, and Trent. Then he turned to Smith.

"Smith," he said, "you were in the tent after Peterson was murdered. Can you tell me how he was lying on his cot?"

"He was lying flat on his back," Smith said.

"Which side of his cot was against the side of the tent?"

"The left side."

Tarzan turned to Ramsgate.

"How long have you known this man Smith?" he asked.

"A few weeks only," replied Ramsgate. "We found him and Peterson wandering around lost. They said their boys had deserted them."

"He was limping when you found him, wasn't he?"

John Ramsgate looked his astonishment.

"Yes," he said. "He told us he had sprained his ankle."

"What's that got to do with it?" demanded Smith. "Didn't I tell you the guy's a nut?"

Tarzan stepped close to Smith.

"Let me have your gun," he said.

"I ain't got no gun," growled Smith.

"What is that bulge underneath the left side of your shirt?" As he spoke, Tarzan placed his hand quickly over the spot.

Smith grinned. "You ain't as smart as you think you are," he said.

Tarzan turned to Lady Barbara.

"Mr. Trent did not kill Burton," he said with great conviction. *"Smith killed him. Smith killed Peterson, too."*

"It's a damn lie!" cried Smith. "You killed 'em yourself! I'm being framed! Can't you all see it?"

"What makes you think Smith is the murderer?" asked Colonel Burton.

"Well, I'll make one change in my statement," said Tarzan. "It was *Campbell* who killed them. This man's name is not Smith. It is Campbell. The real name of the man he killed last night was not Peterson, but Zubanev!"

"I tell you it's a damned lie!" shouted Smith. "You ain't got nothin' on me! You can't prove nothin'!"

Tarzan towered over the rest of the company. A hush fell over the group. Even Smith was silent.

"A very powerful, left-handed man with the second finger of his right hand missing killed Lieutenant Burton," Tarzan said. "The wound which killed Burton could only have been inflicted if the knife were held in the left hand. On his throat were the imprints of a thumb, a first, third, and little finger.

"You will notice that the second finger of Smith's, or rather Campbell's right hand is missing. Also I noticed that when I asked the men to hand me their knives, Campbell was the only man who passed the weapon to me with his left hand. The knife wound in Zubanev's chest was made by a knife held in a left hand."

"But the motive for these murders," exclaimed Romanoff.

"Colonel Burton will find them inside of Campbell's shirt! They are the papers that Lieutenant Burton was carrying when he was shot down by the pursuing plane that carried Campbell and Zubanev. I know that Peterson, or rather Zubanev, was on that plane. The other man with him limped when he walked away from the plane. That man was Campbell, who calls himself Smith."

"But why did Smith or Campbell, or whatever his name is, want to kill Burton and Peterson?" asked John Ramsgate.

"He and Zubanev wanted the papers that Burton carried," Tarzan explained. "No one else knew about the papers. Campbell knew that if he stole the papers and let Burton live, the latter would immediately launch an intensive search through the safari for them. He had to kill Burton. He killed Zubanev so that he would not have to share with him the money that he expected to get for the papers, which they had already tentatively sold to the Italian Government. Here"—Tarzan ripped open Campbell's shirt—"are the papers!"

The native constabulary dragged Joseph Campbell, alias Joe the Pooch, away.

"How did you know that Zubanev was on that Italian plane?" Ramsgate asked curiously.

"I found his glove in the rear cockpit," replied the ape-man.

Ramsgate shook his head in bewilderment.

"I still don't understand," he said.

Tarzan smiled.

"That is because you are a civilized man," he said. "Numa, the Lion, or Sheeta, the Leopard, would understand. When I found that glove I took its scent. Therefore I carried in my memory the smell of Zubanev. Then when I smelled Peterson, I knew he was Zubanev. Hence, Smith must be Campbell. And now—"

Tarzan paused, swept them with his glance.

"I am going home," he said. "Goodby, my friends. It was good to see some of my own people again, but the call of the jungle is stronger. Goodby. . . ."

And Tarzan of the Apes returned to the jungle.